the Black Butterfly

THE BLACK BUTTERFLY INN

the Black Butterfly

THE BLACK BUTTERFLY INN

SHIRLEY REVA VERNICK

Cinco Puntos Press
EL PASO, TEXAS

FIRST EDITION
10 9 8 7 6 5 4 3 2 1

Library of Congress Cataloging-in-Publication Data

Vernick, Shirley Reva.
  The Black Butterfly / by Shirley Reva Vernick. — First edition.
    pages cm
  ISBN 978-1-935955-79-5 (hardback); ISBN 978-1-935955-80-1 (paperback); ISBN 978-1-935955-81-8
  [1. Supernatural—Fiction. 2. Ghosts—Fiction. 3. Hotels—Fiction. 4. Love—Fiction. 5. Mothers and daughters—Fiction. 6. Christmas—Fiction. 7. Maine—Fiction.] I. Title.

  PZ7.V5974Bj 2014
  [Fic]—dc23   2013044152

Book & cover design by Anne M. Giangiulio
With a whole semester off—sort of!

FOR ALAN

Chapter 1

Nothing travels faster than the speed of light
with the possible exception of bad news.

—*Douglas Adams*, THE HITCHHIKER'S GUIDE TO THE GALAXY

One thing you might as well know about me: I'm a collector. Not tacky salt 'n' pepper shakers like my mother or lava lamps like my Uncle Cosmo, who's been stuck in the 1960s for half a century, or smuggled Cuban cigars like my grandfather Quinn. I collect something that's legal and takes up a lot less space: quotes.

I can't say why, exactly, except that I like words. You can do things with words—vent, fantasize, escape, create—and you never have to worry about them walking out on you. They're like having a dog, only without the shedding or the drool. All you have to do is string them together in the right way, and suddenly you're telling a story or changing somebody's mind or even making some kind of difference. I think the day I'll know I've made good in the world is the day I hear someone quoting me.

Mostly I collect famous people's sayings, but I'll hold onto things ordinary people say if they're good enough. Like, just yesterday my sociology teacher said, "Having a family is like having a bowling alley installed in your brain." I don't know if he made it up or if he got it from someone else, but I liked it so I wrote it on my jeans leg. And who knows? Maybe I'll say it myself someday when the situation calls for it.

Today the situation called for something my guidance counselor once said: "Life stinks." All I wanted was to spend Christmas vacation with my own mother in my own house. Was that too much to ask?

Apparently.

It's like this: Mom is in Idaho, 2,500 miles away from our place in Cambridge, Massachusetts. In case you're wondering why on earth she's in the potato state for the holidays, I'll tell you. She's chasing ghosts. Yes, you read that right, chasing ghosts. And if you're thinking *how weird is that*, well, you don't know the half of it. My mother not only believes that "paranormal forces" exist, but she thinks she's going to launch some fabulous new career for herself by catching one on film. All by herself. Like a way, way indie flick. She's the director, producer, camera operator, publicist and host of her so-called documentaries. Her results? Let's say they're less than stellar. In fact, let's say they're nonexistent. But mere constant failure never slows her down. No, nothing as trivial as reality is going to stand between her and her dumbass ideas. So last week when she heard about some ghost haunting a backwoods town out in the wild West, off she went. As usual.

And off I went, as usual, to Mom's best friend Gigi. Gigi has a one-bedroom apartment in Harvard Square over The House of Teriyaki. For the last eight nights, I've been sleeping on her lumpy couch with her four cats, the wail of traffic, and the stink of day-old stir-fry grease. But Mom told me not to worry, that she'd finish up in plenty of time for the holidays.

Then we'd celebrate her masterpiece, which PBS or Nova would undoubtedly scoop up, and things would start looking up for us.

I was actually in a pretty good mood after school today when I went to pick up Gigi at Midnight Brew where she works behind the counter. Mom was due home tomorrow, so I had only one more night on the couch. Plus school break was just around the corner. Right now, the idea of sleeping till noon in my own bed for two whole weeks felt like winning the lottery.

The good mood didn't last long though. I knew something was up as soon as I saw Gigi sitting in the shop's window seat nursing a big styrofoam cup of coffee. She never drinks that stuff, at least not since she started working at this place. Terrible hours, terrible people, terrible uniform—sort of like my life but with minimum wage thrown in. She can't even stand having the smell of joe in her apartment anymore. So she must've really needed the jolt now.

"Hi Geej." I dropped my backpack under the coat rack, which is painted to look like a smiling octopus holding up its tentacles.

"Huh?" Gigi seemed startled by my voice. "Oh, hi Penny. You're early today, aren't you?"

"Nope." I flopped down next to her and waited to see if she'd unload. I figured the chances were 50-50. If she'd just had a fight with her boss or come up short on her cash register, she wouldn't say anything here. But if it had something to do with me, she'd want to say it in a public place, where I couldn't get too...expressive.

I kicked off my clogs and settled into my habit of watching the Harvard kids sip their fancy teas over their iPhones and their poetry books. Gigi peeked at me over the top of her cup and took a big gulp of air. I call this a warning breath. It's what people do right before they say something they know you don't want to hear. They take in an oversized lungful of air and hold it, hoping, I guess, that their bad news will magically disappear by the time they get around to exhaling. Damn, it *was* about me.

"Your mom called earlier," Gigi said, trying to act nonchalant, but I knew a warning breath when I heard one.

"She's not coming home tomorrow, is she." It was a statement, not a question.

I couldn't believe it. I'd literally been counting down the hours until Mom's return. Not because I really thought we'd be rolling in glory. I know the deal by now, how no one will buy or even consider her film, how she'll sit around staring at her toenails until she gets up the oomph to beg for her job at Whole Foods back, and how she'll eventually start snooping around for another lead. Still, I wanted to get back to my own bed, my own clutter, my own life—such as it is.

Gigi didn't say anything, just played with the red velour throw pillow that sat between us, twisting the fringes around her fingers.

"She's not quite wrapped up," I said. "Or she got another lead. Or did she lose her airplane tickets again?" Now my eyes stung.

"I'm sorry," Gigi said, like that was supposed to make me feel all better.

"Am I spending Christmas with you," I asked, "or is she shipping me off to Uncle Cosmo?"

"Cosmo's going to his in-laws in Las Vegas for the holidays.

And I, I'm not going to be around either. I'm going to my sister's this year."

Oh no! That only left Great Aunt Aggie, the world's spittingest, bad-breathiest old maid. Or Cousin Walter, the most gassy, boring loudmouth I've ever had the rotten luck to be related to. "So, how about I cat sit for you?" I offered weakly.

"Penny," Gigi said with a half laugh, "your mom isn't going to let you stay by yourself—or be alone for Christmas. She's made...other plans for you." Her eyes drifted to the floor as she sucked in another warning breath. "Let's go home and you can call her."

Wanting to scream but knowing it might get Gigi in trouble, I went to retrieve my backpack from the octopus. "I hate my life," I muttered as we left.

By the way, this is how your life looks when it's run by someone like my mother: you have to shop for clothes at SecondHand Ro's, and even then, you wait for clearance sales. You take the subway everywhere because there's no car. Your idea of a vacation is a day at the Revere boardwalk. And you move a lot. Never far, just from one crappy apartment to another whenever the rent goes up, just far enough to force you to switch schools every year or two. You don't make friends, so you sit at the outcast table in the cafeteria. You write quotes on your jeans. And you spend a lot of time at Gigi's.

"You hungry?" Gigi asked as we walked in the direction of her apartment. "We could stop at Big Scoops if you want. They have their Christmas flavors out. Peppermint crunch and pecan pie."

"No thanks," I sighed. "I couldn't eat if you paid me, not now."

Mom's bouncing around wouldn't be so bad if there was

The Black Butterfly 11

a dad in the picture, but there isn't. Never has been. All I know about The Donor (a.k.a. Justin) is that Mom met him in Chicago at the Pizza Hut where they both worked part-time. They were in their late twenties, apparently still waiting to bloom. Mom claims they were in love and thought they were going to last forever. Then she decided to go to film school in Boston, and—surprise, surprise—he wouldn't follow her. So she went to Boston by herself—sort of. She was carrying me, only she didn't know it until she got here. She didn't bother telling him. So it's always been just Mom and me, the two of us.

Except when it's just me, alone. And right now, alone felt like my middle name.

Life is divided into the horrible and the miserable.
—Woody Allen

"Mom?"

Static.

"Mom."

"Is that you, Penny? I can barely hear you."

"It's me. How could you do this?"

"Gigi? Penny? Is it Penny or Gigi?"

"When are you coming home, Mom?"

"Didn't Gigi tell you I can't get back on time? Let me talk to her."

"She told me. But when *are* you coming home?" *Not that I ever want to see you again*, I thought.

"What? Penny, speak up. It's terribly noisy in here, and we've got a bad connection."

"Where are you, anyway?" *As if it matters.*

"I'm in Coyote, Idaho. You know that. At the Shotgun Murder Mansion. It's gorgeous out here, honey. I'd love to take you some—"

"Where are you sending me? And for how long?" *You traitor.*

Muffled sounds of chatter.

"Jesus, Mom, can't you go somewhere quieter for half a minute?"

"I'll try. There's a big crowd here waiting to hear the head of the National Paranormal Society speak. Wait now...excuse me, sir. Thank you. Hold on, honey...okay, how's this? I'm outside now. Better? I miss you."

"Look, just tell me what the deal is so I know where I'm gonna be."

"You're going to love it, Penny. At first I was worried. It looked like no one was going to be around this holiday. Then I remembered my old friend Bubbles and *crackle*—said you could *pffffsst*—that Sunday if you want to *crackle*—flight—"

"Mom, you're breaking up. Talk fast before I lose you altogether."

Silence.

"Mom?"

"Penny? Sorry honey, the cell signals are bad down here. I told it all to Gigi before but I'll try again now. I'm going to be here a while longer, so you're going—"

Static. Rapid beeping. Dial tone.

That's how Gigi got stuck telling me Mom's dirty little plan: I'd be spending my Christmas break with Mom's childhood friend Bubbles, someone Mom had never managed to mention, much less introduce me to. Christmas with strangers. Could it get any worse?

Yes, as it turned out, it could. "Where does this Bubbles person live?" I asked, pacing the length of the couch with Tuna Breath kitty at my heels. "Please say Florida, on the beach."

"Well," Gigi said, "it does have a beach." She tried to laugh, but it sounded more like she was gargling. "It's called Islemorow. It's an island, a pretty little island. And it's, it's…"

"Where?"

She wouldn't meet my eyes.

"I'm not going to need sunscreen and tank tops, I take it."

"More like thermals and turtlenecks," she finally confessed, plucking the TV remote from between the cushions and twiddling it. "It's off the coast of Maine, according to your mom. Bubbles runs an inn there. The Black Butterfly Inn. I guess there's a big summer business, but not too many visitors this time of year. So there's space for you. You'll have your own room, at least—that'll be nice. And just think of your poor mother —"

"Oh, yes," I said with all the melodrama I could muster. "My poor, poor mother." *Burdened with that pesky little offspring who has the nerve to expect a roof over her head every night. How does she ever manage?* "So how am I supposed to get to this frozen pebble—swim?"

"Actually," Gigi said, curling her legs under her, "Bubbles is setting up the travel arrangements. You're going to fly there. She must be some friend, that Bubbles, huh?"

I collapsed onto the couch. Tuna Breath pounced on my lap for a cuddle, but I threw him off. He half purred, half meowed, like he wasn't sure how to feel about this unexpected betrayal. My eye caught the famous photo of Mom and Gigi propped up on the end table. They're at Boston's Quincy Market eating ice cream cones, and Gigi is giving Mom a piggyback ride. Gigi is big enough and Mom is short and wiry enough that this is an easy feat for both of them. Mom's frizzy blonde hair takes up half the picture, but your eyes go straight to her legendary smile, complete with ice cream mustache. The two of them look like they're having a blast.

"If this Bubbles is such a great friend," I said, "how come I've never heard of her before? Has Mom ever mentioned her to you?"

"Well no, but—well anyway, it doesn't sound so bad, this place, does it?"

"I'm not going."

"Of course you're going. You have to go." Gigi pushed her plentiful body off the couch and gathered up silky white Boccaccio, her favorite. Boccaccio jumped from her arms straight onto my lap and started rubbing his white whiskers against my cheek. I pushed him away.

"I'm not going," I said again. I stared at the blank TV screen, wondering how Gigi would try to handle me. What could she do, anyway? She couldn't throw me over her shoulder and haul me onto the plane. She could try calling my mother, but even if she got through, what could Mom do all the way from Idaho?

So this is what being in control felt like. And I was. For once in my life, I was in control. No one could make me go to this stinking island if I didn't want to. I could stay right here if

I felt like it. I was in charge, and you know how it felt? Rotten. Because if I didn't go, Gigi would end up skipping her family Christmas to be with me. And when Mom found out, she'd make my life even more miserable than it already was, if that's possible. So I wasn't really in control at all. Mom had won again.

Chapter 2

It's a dangerous business going out your front door.
—J. R. R. Tolkien, THE FELLOWSHIP OF THE RING

Slumped on the subway to Logan Airport, I squinted at the blue-cold day outside and felt frozen to my graffitied plastic seat. There were a few other people in the car, newspapers and paperbacks pressed to their faces. They looked like headless bodies to me, holding their books and papers up not to read but to cover the holes at the tops of their necks. I shouldn't have been surprised. No one with a head on their shoulders would be going where I was.

To distract myself, I dug through my duffel until I found the book I was halfway through reading, *The Adonis Murders*. I love murder mysteries, the more harrowing the better. In fact, I spend so much time at The Poison Pen, a used mystery and suspense bookstore in Central Square, I'm on a first name basis with the owner, Bea, and her resident Yorkie, Laptop. This novel, recommended by Bea herself, was about a string of barbaric murders where all the victims were handsome young men, and it described the corpses in such excruciating detail, I had to skip some passages. Now I was at the part where the detective was receiving death threats at his girlfriend's house, and it felt like the perfect accompaniment to my already dark mood. I opened to the turned down page and plunged in.

At the Airport Station stop, I got off and caught the shuttle the rest of the way to Logan, walking into the terminal—waddling, really, under the weight of my duffel bag—early enough to swing by the coffee bar. Not to buy a five dollar *half decaf extra soymilk single shot of almond cappuccino* like a normal sixteen-year-old. On my budget, all I could do was inhale and hope some secondhand caffeine was floating through the air. I just stood there, visualizing wakefulness, wishing I were somewhere else, and that's when it happened. *It*, as in the one thing that could make this day even worse. *It*, as in Chad Laramy.

Chad is the choicest guy in school: sparkling eyes straight from Tiffany's, black hair hanging irreverently past his ears, a swimmer's body. He's a year ahead of me in school, but we're in the same creative writing class. Not that being in the same room together five days a week means he knows who I am or would ever dream of saying hi to me. Still, in my current natural state (no makeup, no blow dry—hell, I couldn't even remember if I'd put deodorant on this morning), the thought that he might vaguely recognize me was nothing short of terrifying. I tried to move out of the way before he got in line for coffee, but I ended up bumping shoulders with him.

"Whoops," he said. "Sorry."

"No, my fault," I said, hoping there was still time to duck away.

His eyes narrowed. "You look familiar. Do I, do we —"

"Mr. Doyle's writing class."

He flashed his orthodontically perfect smile. "Yeah, that's it. Patty, right?"

"Penny, actually."

"Right. Penny."

"You, um, start your short story yet?"

"Naw," he yawned with out-partying-all-night contentment. "I'll probably whip it out on the plane ride home."

"Me too," I said, even though I'd been working on it for two weeks now. "Well, I liked your last piece, the one about finding your old finger paintings in the attic."

"Thanks," he said, but at this point he was looking past me, not at me, like he was hoping to spot someone more interesting in the terminal to talk to. I wished he'd put me out of my misery and leave, but he just stood there, and I didn't like the silence.

"So…" I fumbled, "you going somewhere for the holidays?"

"Yeah," he said brightly. And why wouldn't he be cheerful? He was surely going on a real vacation. "I'm on my way to Aruba," he said. "You?" Now he was looking straight at me.

Damn, he had to ask. It was bad enough that I had to go to Islemorow. Did I have to confess it to Chad Laramy? "I, I'm going to the islands too," I said.

"Really, which one?" But he was already looking away again. "Oh wait, there's my girlfriend and her mom. Finally, ready to board."

"See you back at Mr. Doyle's then," I said.

"See ya, Patty."

As he walked away, all I could do was wonder: why was it that the only boys who liked me had tails and a litter box? Apparently, that was not for me to know.

The Black Butterfly 19

I boarded the plane only to discover that it wasn't really a plane. It was a glorified kite. I'd never flown before, and I'll admit I was feeling a little jittery. Well, jittery isn't quite the right word—scared sick is more like it.

...*Okay*, I told myself once my teeth stopped chattering. *Okay, we've taken off, and I'm not in the fetal position. I can get through this, I can. After all, what choice do I have, right?*

Somehow, we made it safely to Augusta, Maine, even though I swear the propeller outside my window wasn't rotating. I caught lunch at a vending machine in the airport lobby—M&Ms, the peanut ones (for protein)—and then headed for the puddle jumper that stopped in Waterville, Bangor and Bar Harbor before finally dropping me in Jonesport, where I had to catch a ferry to the island.

The sun was setting on Islemorow by the time the ferry docked, and it was beyond cold. The wind whipped little ice swords at me, and my nostrils froze together in a futile attempt to keep the arctic air out. Thank God the inn's driver was waiting for me at the wharf. He was easy to spot since he was the only one there.

Unfortunately, the driver was in as rotten a mood as me. "Black Butterfly?" he grumbled, winding down the window of his snug minivan, not making eye contact.

I nodded. He didn't look much older than me—eighteen maybe. Wearing no jacket over his thermal shirt, he had longish dark hair, eyes far apart, and a small growth of stubble. His jaw kept flexing, sending little muscular ripples across his cheeks. I found myself wondering what he looked like when he smiled, but no, he wasn't going to be doing that any time soon. Instead, he crammed a fistful of Cheetos into his mouth. "Put your things in the trunk."

Wait a minute, wasn't that his job? I took a step forward to give him a piece of my mind, but what came out of my mouth was, "Could you open the trunk then?" So much for assertiveness.

He heaved an irritated sigh, brushed a Twinkie wrapper off his lap, and rolled out of the car. He was tall and lean in his black jeans.

"Get in," he said after watching me stow my bag. "Don't try to open your window—it's stuck."

"No problem," I said, climbing into the backseat. Like I was going to want more 20-below air slapping me in the face.

"And the seat belts are broken."

"I'm in hell frozen over," I whispered to myself.

"Huh?" he asked as we took off.

"Nothing."

I wiped the frost off my window and looked out at the ragged heaps of snow and bent trees passing by. The road curved sharply at one point, and a few houses appeared. Now, in case you're picturing some quaint New England scene here—shingled cottages with shutters and brick chimneys and tire swings hanging from trees—let me set you straight. These houses looked like trailers minus the wheels, and the yards were piled with rusted cars, broken refrigerators and other junk. I spotted a couple of dogs snooping around an upside down table, and then we were driving through woods.

"How many people on the island?" I asked.

The Black Butterfly

My driver rolled his tongue around his mouth like he was trying to get a piece of Twinkie out from between his teeth. "Depends," he said, peering at me through his rearview mirror. "This time of year, a couple hundred, give or take. Summertime, you can double that easy."

Did he hold my gaze in the mirror for an extra second? Or was it just my imagination? No matter, it didn't matter. Still, I smoothed my hair, which was turning into a frizzy brown mess as the ice melted off it, before pulling myself back into the conversation. "So what do the yearrounders do? For a living, I mean?"

"They catch lobsters," he said, and I knew he wanted to add a *duh*. "Or fix the lobstermen's boats. Or sell food and cigarettes to the lobstermen. Or marry them."

The road twisted again, taking us past an old building that looked like a cross between a diner and a bookshop, or maybe between a convenience store and a library. The pink neon sign said the place was called the Grindle Point Shop. I prayed that it was walkable from the inn. I was going to need something to do during my forced two-week isolation, and maybe the Grindle Point Shop was it.

We drove a short way on, at which point the junk food addict behind the wheel decided to turn on a CD. Loud. Then, just when I thought I'd rather walk the rest of the way, the Black Butterfly Inn appeared before us.

Set back a hundred feet from the road, the inn was a three-story battleship in a sea of snow—grey, weathered, a mishmash of eaves and gables. The front door and windows were crowned with pointed arches straight out of some medieval abbey. From the steep roof, multiple chimneys released tongues of smoke that quickly dissolved into the bitter evening. Maybe the inn was supposed to look like a castle or a church—it was definitely commanding, but in a grim, stiff way, not at all charming or welcoming. If buildings had faces, this one would be puckered up in a frosty snarl, its icicle-shaped holiday lights only making it look colder.

"It's nicer on the inside," my driver said, eyeing me again in the rearview mirror. I wasn't sure I believed him, but somehow it was consoling to learn that the inn didn't dazzle absolutely everyone at first glimpse. Maybe the Black Butterfly scowled at all its visitors. Maybe it even scared some of them. Or maybe this guy was taking pity on the girl who was obviously starting to snap. Either way, I had to admit I appreciated the gesture. And the eye contact.

He drove up the narrow circular driveway but couldn't reach the top because a truck was blocking the way. The truck, a shiny silver job souped up with black racing stripes and oversized chrome wheels, looked out of place against the gothic exterior of the inn. In bold blue print on the tailgate, it said *Mike's Heating and Plumbing—there when you need us.*

"So he finally got around to coming," my driver said, parking directly behind the pickup. "About time." I hoped that meant we'd have heat and water tonight.

A plump woman in a bathrobe and faux fur slippers was standing on the wraparound porch, waving energetically at us. Her hair was a wild shade of red from a bottle, and it matched her lipstick. When I stepped out of the minivan, she ran down the front steps, skirted the pickup, and flung her pudgy arms around me. "Penny!" she cooed. "Penny, at last!" Then she took a step back to examine me. "You're Viv's child, all right."

I gave her my best rendition of a knowing smile.

"I'm Bubbles," she said. "Blanche really, but everyone calls me Bubbles and so should you. I see you've met my son George."

I clamped my jaw to keep it from dropping open. "Yes, we've met. Thanks for the ride, George, and for the tour. That was sweet of you." He pretended he didn't hear me.

Part of me felt sorry for George. If this was his family's business, then he was probably a lifer, sentenced to carting people around in the snow and eating meals out of cellophane bags for the next 60 or 70 years. Talk about lousy luck. But another part of me resented the twit for not letting on who he was. He was the son of the owner. He was the son of my mother's friend. I was going to be spending two weeks with his family. What possible reason could he have for hiding his identity from me? "Mutant," I added under my breath.

That, he heard. "Pardon?" he asked.

I tossed him a big fake smile.

"Let's get you in out of this cold," Bubbles said. "Oh look, it's starting to snow again." She looped her arm through mine and led me to the stairs in short, slippered steps. I felt dizzy all of a sudden. Not dizzy like on a roller coaster, where the downs are always followed by ups. More like the free fall, where it's one freakishly terrifying plummet the whole way. What was I walking into, and why wasn't anyone rescuing me?

I have a new philosophy.
I'm only going to dread one day at a time.
—Charles M. Schulz, Charlie Brown in "Peanuts"

George was right about one thing: the inn *was* nicer on the inside, a lot nicer. The lobby didn't look like any lobby I'd ever seen—no front counter, no tourist posters from the local chamber of commerce, no vending machines. It was more like a den from a fancy house. The paneled walls were hung with oriental rugs of red, gold and blue, and several stained glass skylights studded the cathedral ceiling. A lush brown sectional couch wrapped itself around the fireplace, where a fire crackled and danced. Something about the last bits of daylight mingling with the flames made the air itself seem to flicker and swim.

"Surprised?" teased Bubbles, shaking a set of sleigh bells that rested on a small desk in the corner.

"I live in an efficiency apartment," I explained. "I'm not sure what to do in a place with working thermostats and chairs that don't fold."

She chortled, apparently thinking I was joking. "Glad you like it."

When did I ever say I liked it? I hated this place, hated it. I hated being here, I hated Mom for sending me here, I hated myself for agreeing to come, and no fancy decorations or pretty lights were going to change my mind.

"Here's Vincent then," Bubbles said as an older man

answered her bell. "He'll show you to your room, and we'll get acquainted over dinner, how's that? Vincent, the Lilac Room for Penny, please."

Vincent was a pillowy man with a full head of silver hair framing his baby blues. He wore painter's pants and a down vest, and his belt buckle was a silver and turquoise fish. "Welcome, Miss Penny," he said, picking up my duffel bag.

I followed him across the lobby, through an arched doorway, and into a parlor. This room was bigger and brighter than the lobby—creamy walls with framed mirrors, a marble floor, plenty of recessed lighting. Cushioned armchairs haphazardly lined the walls, and a horseshoe of sofas filled the center of the room.

A girl around my age was sitting cross-legged in one of the armchairs, looking out the bay window. She was pretty—light eyes, light hair, light skin—but I decided not to hold that against her. I was just glad to see there was another guest, someone I might be able to pass some time with on this iceberg. When she looked my way, I nodded and gave a little smile, but instead of smiling back, she jumped out of her chair and ran out of the room. Just my luck—a bizarro. I followed Vincent, wishing the marble tiles beneath my feet would give way to a secret tunnel back to Boston. Regrettably, they only gave way to a curved staircase.

As we climbed to the second floor, Vincent asked, "Do you have plans for your stay?"

Yes, I wanted to say, *I'm planning to die of boredom and loneliness.* But I answered, "I brought a couple of books along. And I have a writing project to finish for one of my classes."

"What are you reading?"

"Right now, a thriller."

"Thriller. Say, did you know Alfred Hitchcock stayed here when he finished *Psycho*, back when the Black Butterfly was new?" he asked. "And Stephen King's wife takes a room almost every Labor Day weekend with her daughter."

"You mean, some mothers actually take their daughters with them when they go away?" I accidentally said this loudly enough for Vincent to hear. He didn't say anything though, and for that I was grateful. I didn't want a pity party or a cheering squad. I just wanted to get through this.

We walked down the hallway, under a crystal chandelier and past garden watercolors. There were four guest rooms on each side of the hall. Instead of room numbers, they had porcelain signs with the rooms' names calligraphed on them. Vincent led us past the Iris, Foxglove, Tiger Lily, Sweet Pea, Indian Pipe, Lady Slipper and Rose rooms, stopping finally at a door half hidden behind a wreath of silk flowers. "Here's the Lilac Room," he said, fishing a key out of his vest and jiggling it in the knob until the door popped open. He handed me the key, then stepped into the blackened room and flipped the wall switch.

Several wall sconces flickered on. My eyes bulged when I saw what the light had to show me: a king-size four-post bed with a sheer canopy and ivory bedding, a stone fireplace flanked by two overstuffed loveseats, and rosy valances swirling their way around a triple window. Lavender brush strokes caressed the walls, while pearly threads of carpeting kissed my feet. And it was all mine. The gods had sent a crumb of justice my way.

"Not bad," I mumbled.

"What's that?" Vincent asked.

"Nothing—sorry." I walked over and sat on one of the loveseats, which felt like velvet and looked like aquamarine—the same color the dancers were wearing in the Degas print hanging over the mantel. "It's just, this room is really pretty."

"It's my personal favorite." He moved past me and set my bag on the chest at the foot of the bed. "Come on," he motioned me over to where he stood. "Take a whiff and tell me what you think."

I didn't know what he was up to, but he must have been trying to cheer me up. Which was a sweet, albeit futile task. Obediently, I walked to the middle of the room and inhaled. The smell was rich, zesty, inviting, like walking into my favorite pizza place. "Wow," I said, "you're right. It smells like...like a feast or something."

"This room sits directly above the kitchen, and *that's* why it's my favorite. Now if you'll allow me, I'll tell you what's for supper. I've got this down to a science, since Miss Rita doesn't let anyone outside the Henion family in her kitchen while she's cooking." He tested the air with several short snuffles at different angles. "Cloves, cinnamon—that's probably the soup. Veal. Some sort of squash—Miss Rita makes a fabulous acorn squash soaked in brandy and mango juice. Let's see, mushrooms and...something nutty for dessert. Sound all right?"

I looked at him, wondering if he were kidding. At home, it's gourmet dining if we bother taking the Spaghettios out of the can. Veal, mangos, dessert? If it weren't for all those hours I spent drooling over the Whole Foods shelves while I waited for Mom to get out of work, I wouldn't even know what real food looked like. I wished I could forget how dismal I felt so I could enjoy this place, but I knew that would never happen. *Nothing fixes a thing so intensely in the mind as the wish to forget it.* That's what some Renaissance guy said about five hundred years ago, and I believe him.

"Supper's at seven," he said, returning to the doorway. "You've got almost an hour. Oh, if you want me to build a fire later, let me know—it's my specialty."

"Okay." I dug into my back pocket, hoping a dollar would show up, but he disappeared before I could tip him.

The first thing I did when I was alone in the room was kick off my clogs and flop belly up on the bed, just looking around, trying to adjust to this alien physical comfort. Satiny sheets, carpeting deep enough to sleep on, a carved table I hadn't noticed on my way in. Everything felt plush and elegant and almost sparkly, but somehow unsettling too. Everything so pristine, so quiet, so someone else's. And here I was, alone in it for the next two weeks.

To busy myself, I decided to unpack. There wasn't much to do, but I managed to make a little project out of hanging up my shirts, stuffing my underwear into the dresser, and unearthing my hair ties. Next, I headed into the bathroom with my toiletry kit.

Wow, the bathroom. Peacock blue tiles from floor to ceiling, black granite countertop, a light-up mirror, Jacuzzi tub, a separate shower stall, and the crowning cherry: a heated floor. I took my time transforming the space into my altar of vanity, laying out all the wares for my skin, hair, teeth and nails. Then I tried to pretend this was my house, that my beauty products weren't drugstore knock-offs, that I padded barefoot on heated floors every day of my life. Yeah, right.

Never eat more than you can lift.
—*Miss Piggy*

"Dinner?" said Vincent from a podium outside the dining room, which was on the far side of the lobby and down a hallway. We were standing in a dimly lit alcove, and he was wearing a suit jacket now. So Vincent was the maître d', as well as the bellhop. Probably the maid and the dishwasher too.

"Come along, Miss," he said, pushing open the door behind him and leading me into a small but lavish room where four glass topped tables stood on four oval rugs. The burgundy walls boasted jewel framed mirrors, bead and ceramic hangings, and an ancient map of the world. A huge picture window and a double fireplace completed the room. It felt dark and spicy in here, old and sophisticated, and I hoped I wouldn't break anything.

Vincent pulled out a high-backed wicker chair for me at the window end of the room. "This is our best table," he noted as I sat down. "The Bushes always request it when they're here from Kennebunkport."

"Bushes?" My disbelief leaked out as a snicker. "As in former Presidents?"

"George, George W, Jeb," he said. "The food is very good here. Very good."

"Oh, I know. I mean, I smell it."

He poured me a glass of water from a crystal pitcher. "Miss Bubbles and George were looking forward to dining with you, but something...came up. I'm afraid you'll have the place to yourself tonight."

What? *Please, Vincent, tell me I heard you wrong.* I couldn't bear the idea of sitting alone through a whole meal here. I felt watched—the glinting eyes of the mirror jewels, the beaded eyes of the wall hangings, the hungry eyes of the sea dragons that swam the oceans of the antique map, they were all on me. I wished my mother were here. I wished this were a real vacation, and we were sitting down to dinner together. But it wasn't anything like that, not even close.

"Where are the other guests?" I asked, hopeful for some other warm bodies in the room.

"You're it," Vincent answered.

"But what about that girl I saw in the parlor?"

"Girl?"

"Blonde hair, jeans, my age?"

Vincent thought for a second and then shrugged. "Don't know who you saw, but honestly, no one else is staying here. Maybe it was Mike the heating guy's daughter. She tags along with him from time to time." He lit the candle in the center of the table, then made a little bow and disappeared into the kitchen.

I dropped my forehead onto my hands and tried to take a few cleansing breaths. *Okay*, I told myself, *this is going to be okay. Who'd want to eat with a strange girl like that, anyway? Or with George No-Personality Henion?* I drank some water from the goblet and began to wonder what could have come up so abruptly. Was George at the bottom of it? Did I disgust him to the point where he refused to come to dinner? A pulse of nausea kicked me in the stomach. All I wanted was to run away, but suddenly Vincent was standing over me again, setting a crock of soup and a loaf of steaming bread on the table.

"A Miss Rita original," he said proudly. "Cream, cinnamon, cloves, beer and five cheeses." He refilled my water and retreated.

Cinnamon and cloves—so he was right. I was still queasy, but I picked up my spoon and played with the soup—stirring, lifting, inhaling, stirring some more. This had to be a week's worth of calories in one bowl—not exactly what I needed. Still, Cook Rita had gone to a lot of trouble, and I didn't want anyone thinking me ungrateful, so I put a spoonful to my mouth.

Whoa. This was good. Very good, as Vincent said. I ate the rest of the spoonful greedily, then promised myself that would be all.

I broke my promise. This velvet potion was some kind of magic. I was suddenly ravenous, and a pinch less afraid of the room. If I didn't look up at the eyes all around me, I could pretend they weren't staring.

At one point, Vincent approached with a salad, but he withdrew when he saw I was still working on the soup. I'd have made that soup last until morning if I could, but when Vincent appeared with the salad for a second time, he insisted that I not fill up on the first course.

The salad. Wilted kale, Vincent explained, and roasted potatoes with plenty of garlic, topped off with a luscious tahini dressing. Who needed a main dish after all this? I did, I realized—once the veal and brandied squash arrived. I don't know who ever thought up brandied vegetables, but I'd like to shake their hand.

I had no room at the end for the dessert, a creamy, nutty, not quite cake, not quite pastry thing that called to me from the center of a chocolate-drizzled plate. All I could do was nibble lovingly at the pistachios and the cocoa powder. The finale was an espresso served in a little Art Deco cup. Lingering over it, I knew Mom might be having more adventures than me right now, and Chad Laramy might be getting a better tan in Aruba, but no one was getting a better supper.

When I finally set my linen napkin on the table and pushed my chair back, I checked my watch. Nine o'clock. I'd spent two full hours here. That's like ten normal dinnertimes for me. How did that much time go by?

As I left the dining room, I planned to head straight upstairs, but the caffeine hit me by the time I reached the parlor. Then I remembered a room I'd passed in the hallway on my way to and from dinner, a little room lined with bookshelves and crowded with armchairs and a sofa. A study, I guessed, or a lounge. Maybe it would have some decent magazines to help me while away my wakefulness or even some boring ones to put me to sleep. I turned around.

The study, softly lit by two table lamps, was windowless, which was a bonus. In here, I could pretend it wasn't winter outside. I could pretend it wasn't even Maine outside. This could be the study in some Caribbean retreat. Chad Laramy might be right next door. I liked this room—I didn't even mind being alone in it—and I had the feeling I'd be spending a lot of time here in the long days ahead.

The bookshelves were loosely organized by category: travel, spiritual, food, boats, paperback novels, even comic books. I stopped at the paperback section, hoping to find a mystery I hadn't read yet. I hadn't read any of them. They were all wonderfully old, outdated and heavily thumbed. *Six Parts Joy, One Part Murder* caught my eye, and I took it out. The back flap promised a lurid tale of grisly crimes and a first-rate gumshoe—my kind of story. Just as I was turning to the first page though, a loud blare behind me nearly stopped my heart. I spun around and pressed my back against the shelves.

The face of a woman peered from around an armchair. Its high back had hidden her from my view. "Hello," she said in a slight accent—French, I thought—and then she sneezed thunderously twice more. "I am sorry to startle you."

"No, no," I panted, heading to the sofa. "I just didn't see you there." *Plus I thought I was the only guest.*

At least old enough to be my mother's mother, this woman wore jeans and a loose sweater and sat with her legs curled under her, a thick book crooked in one arm. With tawny eyes, milky skin and silver hair, she'd clearly once been beautiful, and, in fact, still was. I hoped I'd like my elegant inn mate, whoever she was, since we were bound to be tripping all over each other in the confines of the inn.

"How was supper tonight?" she asked.

"Great." I patted my belly, wondering why she hadn't eaten. Maybe she'd only just checked in. Maybe she was an unexpected arrival. "Really outstanding."

"No, it was not. It was bland—mediocre at best."

The hair on my nape bristled. I felt personally attacked by this insult to the closest thing to nirvana I'd ever tasted. "I don't think we had the same thing," I said, wondering where and when she'd eaten, if not in the dining room at the appointed hour. "Did you have the veal?"

"No. I cooked it. I am Rita, the chef." And then she smiled.

This was Miss Rita? I'd imagined someone bigger, more Italian, wearing white and smelling of oregano. It took me a second to adjust to the reality. "Penny," I said at last.

"I know."

"Oh. Well, I thought everything was fabulous. Especially the soup. And the dessert—I should have saved room."

She smiled broadly, the lines at her temples crinkling into crescents. "I am glad it was all right. You know, I can hardly get anything fresh, really fresh, out here this time of year. All I can do is improvise."

"But it was wonderful, really."

"I am glad. So, what are you reading?"

"Pure pulp," I said, feeling a little embarrassed about my choice of literature. "How about you?"

"A cookbook." She held up *Cuisine Under the Stars*. "It is how I sustain myself in the dreary winter. I decide what I would make if I could get the ingredients. Then I am not so sad about waiting. Let me tell you what would have been on tonight's menu, no?"

I nodded.

"Since I did much of my training in Brussels," she started, "I would prepare a Belgian supper, goose *a l'instar de Vise*. It is only worth bothering with if you can find a fresh young bird, in springtime." Rita described how she'd quarter the goose and simmer it in a garlic and white wine broth brimming with celery, carrots, onions and spices fresh from the garden. Next, she'd fry the bird golden crisp in a batter of eggs and crumbled homemade bread. Then she'd dribble a sauce of mashed garlic, broth, egg yolks, heavy cream and butter over it. "Flemish asparagus, just picked, and boiled potatoes on the side and *voilà*."

I think I actually whimpered, but at least I didn't drool.

"And for dessert," she went on, "*gaufres Bruxelloises*. Waffles cooked in a pint of beer for crispness, sprinkled with brown sugar and topped with butter."

"Sounds amazing," I said.

"And you?"

"I'm sorry?"

"What would you make for supper?" She tried to hand me her cookbook.

"No, no. The only poultry I handle has been precooked by Frank Perdue."

"But you can imagine."

So I did. Leafing through her cookbook, I used the photos to create a four-course meal of scallop and mussel bisque, mesclun and persimmon salad, grilled tenderloin with papaya chutney, and something called chocolate melting cake. Not that I'd ever eaten these dishes before, but the words tasted delicious as I spoke them.

"*Bien!*" Rita clapped her hands when I finished presenting my menu. "Good!"

After that, she asked what my all-time most memorable meal was. "Tonight's supper, definitely," I said. "And you, what was your favorite?"

She sat back and rested her head against the armchair, gazing at one of the table lamps. She looked far away, as if she were reliving a memory instead of just trying to put her finger on one. Finally she said, "It was a tuna and potato chip casserole. Tuna, from a can. And the potato chips were stale." She laughed to herself, still staring at the memory hovering above the lamp.

"That must've been some recipe," I said.

"No, the recipe was silly. But the cook, *he* was extraordinary."

"He?"

"Now tell me. Tell me who you would invite to a dinner party. If it could be anyone, anyone at all."

Okay, so she didn't want to spill about the guy. All right, fine, for now. "Anyone?" I asked. "Even people from the past?"

"Certainly."

For some reason, the first person I thought of was George Henion. What was I thinking? Why would I want to break bread with a guy who either didn't know how to talk or who didn't want to talk to me specifically? "I guess I'd want to have some of my favorite novelists," I said, "like Dean Koontz and Patricia Cornwell and Kurt Vonnegut. And, well, I wouldn't mind hanging out with Johnny Depp or Channing Tatum. Oh, and the Dalai Lama—he's got a great smile. I'd put him at the head of the table. Then I'd sit between Johnny and Channing, and the writers, they could all sit across the table from me…is that ridiculous?"

Rita shook her head. "Not compared to my wish list."

"Why? Who's on it?"

She looked at me blankly for a moment. "Not too many people. Just my father when he was a boy. My mother as a young woman. My sister as she was the last time I saw her. Myself when I am very old. And you too, I think. Yes, when you are my age now. We would have a lovely time, all of us."

"What about the man who made you the tuna and chips casserole?"

"Ah, you are a clever one. Another time I will tell you about him, maybe. But now I must get some sleep if I am going to make real food tomorrow." She uncurled her legs and stood up. "Good night, dear. My room is right next door, if you need anything."

"Night, Rita. Thanks for dinner. And the talk."

After she left, I stayed on in the study to read, happy to have made a friend here at Chez Strange. I'd never had a friend who came from another generation or another country. Come to think of it, I'm not sure I ever really had a genuine friend before, someone to share food fantasies and guest lists with, someone to just laze an evening away with. So this was exciting—pitiful, but exciting.

By the time I got through the first few chapters of *Six Parts Joy, One Part Murder*, it was almost one o'clock. I still wasn't tired, but I decided to go to my room anyway—might as well enjoy the canopy bed and fancy pillows while I had the chance. I left the study and went down the hall, across the parlor, up the curved staircase and past the garden watercolors. It seemed like a long walk. By the time I reached my door, I felt like maybe I'd be able to sleep soon.

Well, you made it through your first day, I told myself as I headed to the bathroom to perform my bedtime purification rite. *One down, thirteen to go.* Actually, if the rest of my stay could be half as pleasant as the evening I'd just spent with Rita, I'd be all over this gig. But that was never going to happen—my luck doesn't roll like that. I sighed and pulled on my pajamas and fuzzy socks.

We have a dollhouse-size bathroom mirror at home, so I wasn't used to seeing such a complete, brightly lit view of myself. I wasn't sure I liked the full-size image. Honestly, I'd happily suffer the eyebrow plucking and the occasional zits, if only they'd come along with a decent chest. But here I was, with a body that hadn't kept pace with my social aspirations, fumbling for my tweezers and Clearasil, wishing for fuller lips and more mysterious eyes. Oh well, who was I going to try to impress around this godforsaken place, anyway?

When I climbed into the canopy bed a few minutes later, the sheets, though luxurious, felt cold and a little rigid—or was that just me? It was probably just me. I forced myself to lie still, and sleep eventually overtook me.

Chapter 3

DECEMBER 20

Getting out of bed in the morning is an act of false confidence.
—Jules Feiffer

Having stretched my stomach out at supper, I was naturally
starving the next morning. The dining room door was ajar,
and I could see that the room was empty. Then I noticed an
envelope with my name on it taped to the maître d's podium.
It was a woman's handwriting, and for an instant I thought
it was my mother's. She'd come to her senses, she'd realized
what she'd done to me, and she was on her way here to beg
my forgiveness.

No, that couldn't be it. Mom wasn't diverting a single
neuron to thoughts of her own flesh and blood. I slid a finger
under the flap and pulled out the paper, Black Butterfly
letterhead covered with flowery fountain pen handwriting:

Penny dear,

> *So sorry about dinner last night. Will explain*
> *later. I'm off to an appointment on the mainland.*
> *Breakfast is buffet-style, and I trust that by the time*
> *you find this note, the food will be out. Enjoy.*

I hope to be back by late afternoon or suppertime
at the outside. If you need anything in the meantime,
Vincent will be happy to help.
So glad you're with us —
Bubbles

For someone who was so glad I was here, she was doing a
darn good job of making herself scarce. Just like Mom. And
while we're at it, where had George managed to hide himself
since yesterday afternoon? Whatever was making the Henions
disappear all the time, I didn't like it. Not that I'm normally
averse to being by myself—I've gotten used to that over the
years—but this was getting ridiculous. Well, if I had to be alone,
I might as well be alone in a room full of good food.

Towering with fresh fruit, grains, plus all things decadent,
the buffet table was a page out of some slick gourmet magazine,
and a good distraction. The food, the tablecloth, the china,
the silk flowers—all this, just for me? At least *someone* seemed
to care. I put some pineapple chunks, a strip of bacon, and a
cranberry muffin on a plate.

I went to the same table I'd had last night, between the
picture window and the fireplace. In the light of day I could
see out the window, and I stared at the cloud covered world
before sitting down. Ice-plated armor encased the evergreen
bushes hugging the backside of the inn. Beyond, a flat expanse
of snow stretched until, a few hundred yards out, it gave way to
a steel grey sea. Not a single bird or squirrel skittered around
the grounds. Maybe they didn't live this far north. "Oh, God," I
groaned. I had to endure thirteen more days in a wasteland that

even critters with acorn-sized brains knew enough to avoid. I fell into my seat.

I'd just put the bacon to my lips when I heard a "good morning" from behind. I turned around to see Rita. Thank God, a friendly face. "Morning," I said.

"May I?" Rita asked, pointing to the empty chair across from me.

"Of course."

Today Rita was wearing a coral sweater that brought out the bit of pink I hadn't noticed in her cheeks last night. Her grey corduroys made a trim line down to her suede flats. I hope I'm half that chic when I'm her age.

"I am wondering, would you like to help me today?" she asked.

"Help you?"

"Yes, help me to bake."

I was so delighted to have an invitation to spend time with Rita—with anyone, really, but especially with her—I almost forgot to be confused. "But wait, Vincent told me you don't let anyone in your kitchen when you cook, except for the family."

"That is right, usually. But you and I, we are—how do you say—kind spirits, yes?"

"Kindred spirits, I think you mean."

She inched back her chair. "Shall we then?"

"Let's do it."

"Today we make *pain d'amandes*," she said, standing up. "Take your plate, if you like."

"Pen what?" I asked as I followed her across the dining room.

"*Pain d'amandes*. It means almond bread, but it is really a cookie made of everything sweet—honey, brandy, brown sugar, almonds."

Rita pushed the swinging door, and suddenly we were in her kitchen. Now, don't picture one of those oversized, steel industrial kitchens that reek like a school cafeteria. This room was snug, all white and blue tiles, with a wooden floor, a large skylight, and the aroma of Tollhouse cookies. Rita went straight to the pantry—a room in itself off to the left—and emerged a minute later loaded with baking supplies. I watched her stack the center island with spices, sugars, a jar of nuts, and all kinds of utensils. The island, part butcher-block, part tile, housed a deep sink and a gas stove that already had a pot bubbling on it.

"You like this space?" she asked.

"I love it."

"A little small for a working kitchen, but I make do with what I have." She tied on an apron, a yellow one with the words *Etoile Rouge* stitched at the top. Then we both washed our hands.

"We blanch the almonds first," she explained. "That means we take the brown skin off."

I picked a nut out of the jar. "Do we use a knife?"

"No," she laughed, "we boil them." She took the jar from me and poured the nuts into the boiling pot. The water hissed and jumped up at her and then calmed into a rippling simmer. "These are ready now," she said after a few seconds, taking the pot from the stove and draining the water into the sink. She picked up a single steaming almond and slipped her thumbnail under the puckering skin, which slid away to reveal the creamy meat within. "You try," she said, tossing the nut into a bowl and taking another.

This had to be one of those things that looked a lot easier than it was, like on those cable cooking shows. I picked up a warm nut and examined it, hoping to find some hidden zipper to part the skin. Failing that, I tried Rita's technique and—eureka!—I was holding a blanched almond. "Hey, this really works," I said. But Rita was already sifting flour and cinnamon into a bowl and stirring in clumps of brown sugar, so I kept working.

When I finished peeling the nuts, Rita used a rounded blade to chop them. Then she added the nuts to the flour mixture, along with butter, brandy, honey and milk—all in no particular measure, just feeling her way. "Now we work the dough," she said, stepping back to let me in.

I had no idea what it meant to work dough, so I stood there feeling and probably looking dumb.

"With your fingers," Rita explained. "Until it is like clay." She took my hands and pushed them into the dough. Her fingers felt strong and sure of themselves. "Relax. This is the fun part. Pretend you are a child in mud. Play with it."

I plunged my fingers deeper into the dough, feeling the grit of the almonds and the silk of the butter against my skin. Just like mud, only without the earthworms. The more I mixed and scrunched, the stronger the fragrance, until I could almost taste the brandy.

"This is good, yes?" Rita said.

"This is good, yes."

"Now we shape it into a ball. You let me do this. Very

sticky." She rubbed her hands with flour before dumping the dough onto the butcher block and forming the blob into a sphere. "There."

"So now we bake?" I asked, eager for our creation to take its final form.

"No." She carried the ball to the fridge, a coppery Sub-Zero number. "Now we chill. Tomorrow we bake. But if you like, we could start on something else. Hold on, let me get some things. I have an idea." She gave me a quick smile and disappeared into the pantry.

No sooner was Rita out of sight than George ambled into the kitchen. He was wearing faded blue jeans with a small hole that offered a peek at his muscular thigh. His navy sweatshirt said C.I.A. in large white letters. He still needed a shave, but his hair was freshly washed and drying wavy. Stopping short when he spotted me, George's mouth opened, but no words came out. I knew what he was thinking though: there was a non-Henion in the kitchen. I felt the blood color my cheeks.

Suddenly Rita was standing next to me. "I could not find what I needed, I am afraid," she said. "Oh, hello, George. Penny and I had important work here this morning." She winked at me.

George folded his arms and took me in. With daylight on his face, I was getting my first good glimpse of his eyes, only I couldn't tell what color they were. Either bluish green or greenish blue. No, that wasn't it. He turned his head slightly, and then I got it. His eyes were two different colors—one green, one blue, like a peridot and a sapphire, or maybe jade and lapis. He uncrossed his arms long enough to rub his neck—did my stare make him uneasy?—and a necklace spilled out from under his shirt. It was a crescent moon-shaped pendant with a stone the same shade of blue as his right eye. Dangling from a slender gold chain, it looked like an expensive piece of jewelry, and I had to wonder if it was from a girl.

"George, can I get something for you?" Rita asked.

"Maybe a—"

"No, nothing," he said, still looking my way. "I was just going to…but never mind. I didn't realize the kitchen was in use."

"Actually, I was just leaving," I said. And it was true. As soon as he showed up, I decided I was just leaving.

"No, no," he insisted. "You finish up your—whatever it is. I'm not really hungry anyway. I'm…yeah." He about-faced and walked out the door without another word.

"What's the matter with him anyway?" I asked after the door swung closed behind him. "I mean, what've I ever done to him?"

Rita wiped her wrists on her apron, leaving two floury splotches. "Do not take it personally, my dear. He gets big headaches—migraines—that is all."

But I didn't believe that was all. Something wasn't right. Bubbles treating me like her long lost godchild. George treating me like a leper. Not to mention the fact that Mom never so much as uttered the Henion name before last week.

"There's something else, isn't there?" I said.

"Something else?" Rita made a point of not looking up.

"Something I did. Or something I said. Maybe just being here, cutting into George's space."

"I think…" she started. "No, I do not know."

"Don't you?"

She shook her head. "Perhaps I have said too much already."

"Rita—"

"I know you have a curious mind, but some of the things you wish to know are not for me to tell."

"But we're kindred spirits, you and me, right?"

She pinched her lips shut.

"It's just—I'm all alone here, and I don't know what's going on. If you could just throw me a lifeline..."

Still no response.

"You know what?" I said. "I'm sorry. This is obviously a sensitive subject. I'm sorry if I intruded." Confession time: this is a ploy Mom taught me. When someone resists answering your question, you apologize for having asked. That usually guilts the person into answering. They feel sorry for having put you in an awkward position, even though you're the one who actually put them in a difficult spot.

"Okay, all right, you have me," Rita said. "Come, sit."

Bingo. I dropped onto a stool while Rita stood leaning against the island, looking uneasy. "Penny," she said, fumbling with her apron strings, "do you have any idea why Bubbles and your mother are no longer best friends?"

"They were best friends?"

"They were very close. But when your mother called to ask if you could stay here, they had not spoken for a long time—years."

"Oh, God, what did Mom do?"

Rita sat on the edge of the stool next to mine. "Your mother came to visit one summer when I was still fairly new here. And what happened was..." She drew a warning breath.

"What happened was, your mother got the idea that the inn was haunted. She said the TV kept turning on all by itself, that the phone in her room would ring, but no one would be there when she answered it. Things like that."

I stifled a moan.

"Your mother thought it was wonderful. She wanted to—how you say—promote the 'haunted inn.' She called the newspaper. She called a TV station on the mainland."

"Poor Bubbles."

"Now, for some reason, your mother thought the crawlspace had something to do with the ghost—there is a crawlspace right over here, behind that potted plant. So one afternoon when the kitchen was empty, she went into the space to have a look, which would not have been so terrible except that she left the door open. Little George—he was just a toddler—wandered into the crawlspace. Climbed the stairs inside. Fell. And ended up at Jonesport Hospital with a concussion and a gash on his forehead." She pointed to her eyebrow.

I winced. How could Mom have been so careless, so thoughtless?

Rita stood up and began filling the sink with dish soap. "Your mother left the very next day. As far as I know, the two of them did not talk again, until last week."

I spun around to face her. "So George has spent his life hearing the story of the nut who got him hurt then."

"Not so," Rita said. "Bubbles never talked of it. And George does not remember the accident. No, I do not think George knew anything, not until last week when your mother called and Bubbles got a little crazy. Who knows what she finally told him? But, well, I imagine it makes him…"

"…suspicious? Like I'm picking up the ghost trail where she left off? Rita, you've got to believe me. I didn't know about any of this. If I did, I'd've run away from home rather than show my face here…did he go ballistic when he found out I was coming?"

"You wish to know all the details. I understand. But later. Tonight, in the study." She tipped her head toward the door.

I was dismissed.

The universe is made of stories, not atoms.
—*Muriel Rukeyser*

With nowhere else to go, I went back to my room, where I attempted to distract myself by reading, working on my short story assignment, checking out the furniture. Whenever I peeked out the window, I saw Vincent shoveling the back walk or carrying in firewood from the shed. Later, dinner smells started wafting through the floorboards, and I knew Rita was directly below me. Nice, but not nice enough to ward off my boredom and loneliness, much less my outrage at Mom.

For the first time ever, I found myself wishing I knew more about Mom's past. As it was, I'd only heard a couple of her stories, none of them firsthand. From Grandpa Quinn, I knew she collected imaginary friends worryingly late into childhood. From Uncle Cosmo, I learned about her stash of books on the occult. And from Great Aunt Aggie, I found out about Mom's infamous high school career. It didn't start out so bad, actually.

The Black Butterfly 49

In fact, when she was a sophomore, she got an academic scholarship to some chichi private school on the North Shore of Boston. Things were okay there until her Spanish class took a trip to Mexico junior year. P.S., Mom got sent home early with the "suggestion" that she seek "other educational opportunities." So what went down in those Mexican ruins—boys, drugs? Whatever it was, Mom was sufficiently unnerved that to this day she won't talk about it.

Apparently, she wasn't so unhappy about the expulsion though. She gladly traded her pleated skirt uniform for a pair of grungy jeans, hopped the city bus for the crowded public school, and joined the photography club that met at the local library. Wait, was it the photography club or the paranormal club? I couldn't remember. I knew my mother better than I knew The Donor, but I didn't really know her, not by a long shot.

Just as the afternoon sun was taking its last gasp, the phone on my nightstand rang—loudly—and I jumped up. "Hello?"

"Hi honey, it's Mom."

Mom, oh God! Should I confront her about what I now knew? Should I make her admit that she dropped me in the middle of the minefield she planted all those years ago? I was dying to tackle her on this. I was furious with her, and I needed her to know it.

"Honey?" she repeated.

"Right here, Mom."

"How are you settling in? You'll never guess where I am."

"Aren't you still in Idaho?"

"Yes, of course, but wait till you hear this. I'm in Boise, the capital, and I'm at the big radio station here. I'm going to interview the owner of the Shotgun Murder Mansion *and* the President!"

"The President?"

"Of the Paranormal Society, silly. Right after he does a call-in show about the sighting at the mansion, he's going to talk to me. Can you believe it?"

"No kidding."

"Anyway, what about you? And Bubbles? How is she?"

"To tell the truth, I haven't seen much of her yet. We're having supper together tonight, so I guess I'll—"

"Get her to tell you about our old bra designing contests," Mom giggled. "She'll have you peeing in your pants…oh my golly" (I swear, she actually said 'oh my golly'), "I think I just saw the President walk by. It must be almost show time. I should probably—"

"No, Mom, don't go yet. We need to talk." A zap of static came over the line. "Mom?"

"Right here, honey. What's up? Is everything all right?"

I collapsed onto the bed. "No, everything is not all right. Everything is awful. Why didn't you tell me? Why didn't you at least warn me about you and Bubbles, about what happened, how you haven't talked in years?"

"Well, I—"

"Jesus, why did you send me to a place where we're *persona non grata*?"

"Persona non grata—what are you talking about, Penny? Someone has you thinking I'm on the outs?"

"Spare me the act, Mom. I know all about the crawlspace accident."

There was a short silence on the line followed by more static.

"Mom, are you still there?"

"It's my battery, I think—it's starting to go. Look, I want to tell you something before this phone dies completely. It's true that when I phoned Bubbles last week, we hadn't talked in, what, sixteen, seventeen years. But it's not my fault. It's not anything I did."

I didn't respond.

"Penny, did you hear me?"

"I heard you. I just, I don't think I believe you."

She made an almost laugh. "Let me get this straight. You're going to believe someone you just met over your own mother?"

"I guess you're going to have to convince me. Convince me that there's some other explanation."

"I will not," she barked. "It's nothing I want to talk about, nothing I've ever told anyone, and I'm certainly not going to start by telling you. If it's details you want, I'm sorry. I'm not going there."

"Fine."

"Fine."

"I guess there's nothing else to talk about then. Goodbye, Mom."

"Penny, wait. Let's not end like this. I hate to hear you so upset."

"Then help me."

"Not the way you're asking me to help you. Let's try—"

"Goodbye." I hung up, feeling more miserable than ever. It was bad enough that Mom omitted vital information before sending me here. But now, to lie about it when I asked, that was unforgiveable. She really must not give a damn about me.

I was thinking very seriously about having myself a good cry—I was already looking around for some tissues—when there was a knock at my door. Wiping my eyes on the back of my hand, I pulled myself up off the bed and answered it.

I found a nice-looking guy leaning against the doorframe. Thick black hair hung over his chestnut eyes, and a few freckles punctuated his caramel face. He wore work boots, jeans and a maroon flannel shirt. He wasn't much taller than me, but his athletic build made him look bigger.

"I'm here to double-check the windows," he said. "The temperature in some of the rooms is a little low, and we're trying to figure out why. Is this a good time?"

So Vincent had some help around the place—good. "Sure," I said, waving him in.

"I'm Blue," he said.

"Join the club."

"No, I mean, my name is Blue."

"Oh, right. Sorry. Penny," I said and stuck out my hand.

Instead of shaking it, he went straight to the windows and ran his fingers along the frame. "Good to meet you." He pulled a screwdriver out of his pocket and began fiddling with the latches. "I don't see any problems here, but I'll tighten things up just to be sure."

"Great, thanks."

"All set," he said after a minute. He turned around, twiddling the screwdriver between his fingers. "See you around then, I guess." He smiled then and when he did, his eyes shimmered, as if backlit from behind. It threw me off guard, and I didn't speak. "Right," he said and let himself out.

Conversation is the enemy of good wine and food.
—*Alfred Hitchcock*

Bubbles showed up at the dining room by herself, claiming that George was sleeping off a "nasty something." She assured me she'd given him a hefty dose of Echinacea and ordered the poor boy to bed.

A different table was set tonight, this one closer to the kitchen and farther from the fireplace. "I hope you don't mind, dear," Bubbles said as we sat down. "That fire makes me sweat." She was wearing a hot pink sweater over black stretch pants that hugged her a little too tightly. In place of her faux fur slippers she wore mules, and every time she turned her head, her feather earrings swayed. I see this outfit a lot on the Revere boardwalk—the New England trash look.

It was nice to have a dinner companion, though I didn't know how to begin a conversation with Bubbles. There was no menu to discuss. There'd been no change in the weather, good or bad. I wanted to know why she'd missed last night's dinner but didn't want to ask outright. And of course I was dying to know what George's deal was, but no, I couldn't ask that either. So I decided to wait for her to speak. And did she ever! That woman could talk. During the first course—these amazing spicy meatballs that Vincent called *vitoulets*—Bubbles described her short-lived stint as a professional party planner. Over the palate cleanser—ice water for me, a whiskey sour for her—she rhapsodized over some band called The Big Stuck. This segued into a monologue about the entertainment industry, which took us straight through the salad course—braised endive with black currants and Cajun crabmeat.

While Bubbles nursed her second mixed drink, I decided to take the plunge. "So Bubbles, how long have you known my mom?"

"Gosh, must be about, what, almost thirty years now."

"Did you meet in school?"

"No," she said, playing with her paper umbrella. "We never lived in the same state. We worked summers together at a kids' camp. She…didn't tell you?"

"No."

She shifted in her seat. "I see."

"That's just not her style, Bubbles, that's all."

"I guess."

"I bet she didn't tell you much about me either, right?"

She smiled a small smile. "Then it's up to us to fill each other in. Good thing we've got a couple of weeks."

"I won't need nearly that long to tell you about me. I'm not that interesting."

"Nonsense," she said emphatically. "I have all sorts of questions for you."

Before she got any questions out though, Vincent appeared with the main course, which he needed both arms to deliver. I'd never seen anything like it. Picture a tray with concentric circles of increasingly intense color and texture, starting with mussels and including caramelized shallots, fat shrimp, tangy mushrooms, scallops, cherries, fennel sausages, pomegranate pulp and tons of grilled root vegetables. It was bliss on a plate. Bubbles and I hardly talked while we demolished it, which I was thankful for since I really didn't want to be interrogated.

During our after-dinner tea—well, I had tea, Bubbles had cognac—her sleeve fell back just enough to reveal a bracelet. It was thick and wide and colorful and intricate. "What a great bracelet," I said, glad to find some part of her outfit that I could compliment honestly. "Did you get it around here?"

"This? I made it." She held her wrist up to give me a closer look, then beamed, "I'm so tickled you noticed it."

"It's a knockout. Hey, what's this?" I asked, reaching over the table to touch a sparkly red charm.

"Glass, from an old earring I had. I have a little business making jewelry out of recycled glass and old machine parts. See this?" She pointed to a bumpy metal square. "That's a chip from George's first computer."

"Charm-ing," I said, feeling a little dumb at the bad pun, but happy to make her laugh after the awkward business about Mom. I considered asking if she'd made the crescent moon necklace George was wearing this morning, but something told me not to. That necklace had girlfriend written all over it. Instead I asked, "Do you sell your things in stores?"

"Well, I have a few things at the counter at the Grindle Point Shop down the road. I'm trying to get my favorite jewelry store in Bangor to take some things on consignment. But mostly I go to church bazaars or give them as gifts. You really like it?" she said, holding the bracelet up so the candlelight caught the glass.

"Really. So, what do you call yourself? I mean, your business?"

Bubbles leaned forward and lowered her voice, as if she were about to divulge some highly confidential corporate secret. "I'm toying with calling myself One Man's Trash is Another Man's Treasure."

I nodded and tried to look impressed, although I thought this name was completely off target. What was she thinking, calling her artwork trash and referring to it as a *man's* treasure? And how did she ever expect to fit all those words onto a jewelry-sized gift box or a business card? Still, she seemed attached to it, and I didn't want to burst Bubbles' bubble.

She scooted her chair closer to mine. "I'm so happy you're here, Penny. Thank heavens your mother thought to call on me. Finally, to talk again after all that old...business."

"Y-yes."

"So, that much you do know about me—the unpleasant parts."

This was going nowhere good fast. "It's not like that, Bubbles. It's just—"

"No, no need to explain, dear." She took another gulp of her cognac. "I'm just so glad to be back in touch. You know, I tried to salvage the friendship—after things calmed down a bit, of course—I really did. But your mother was off in other directions, and I finally gave up. What else could I do? And then, lo and behold, I pick up the phone last week and it's her. It's Vivian, sounding just like she did all those years ago."

"That's Mom for you."

She smiled, and then the smile morphed into a large yawn.

"And now I really must trundle myself off to bed. Thank you, dear, for a delightful evening." She pushed back her chair and took the last swig of her drink. Standing up, she had to brace herself against the table for balance. "My, I didn't realize quite how...sleepy...I am. Pleasant dreams, now." Before I could say another word, she was staggering toward the door.

"I could walk you to your room," I called, but Vincent arrived all at once, taking her arm and ushering her out of the room. Actually, I was glad to avoid escort duty. I had an important rendezvous with Rita to get to. I was going to get her to tell me all about Mom and Bubbles.

I can have oodles of charm when I want to.
—*Kurt Vonnegut,* BREAKFAST OF CHAMPIONS

I got to the study before Rita, so I took *Breakfast in Brazil* off the bookshelf and parked on the sofa to wait. And wait. And wait some more. I went through *Snacking in Tuscany* and *Vegan Riviera* too, but still no sign of Rita. I leafed through an atlas that was so old it showed Alaska belonging to Russia. I tried out every chair. Where could she be? Did she forget? It was ten o'clock already. Had I gotten here too late or too early? Was I in the wrong room? Then, just as I got up to put the books away, I heard footsteps, and George walked in.

I dropped one of the books. On my foot. George looked as dazed to see me as I was to see him.

"Hello," I mumbled, picking up the book and thinking I'd just slip past him and be on my way.

"Hello," he said stiffly, not making eye contact. He'd shaved since I saw him last, and now I saw the dimples. "Feeling better?" I asked.

"Lousy headache. I get them. Then all I can do is hole up in a dark room and pray for sleep."

"Too bad you had to miss dinner. Again."

"I'm not very good company when I'm in pain. You probably noticed that."

"Yeah, well..." Maybe it was his headache, maybe it was whatever Bubbles told him about Mom. Either way, he had plenty of reason to keep to himself.

He didn't say anything else, and there was nothing left for me to say, so I walked out of the room. I figured my best hope with George was for peaceful coexistence, and that translated into keeping my distance. But before I'd taken more than a few steps in the direction of the parlor, he poked his head out. "Hey," he said. "I'm gonna scrounge around for some leftovers. You...uh...wanna come?"

Wait a minute, did I hear right? It sounded like George just invited me along. Bubbles must have pressured him into making nice, or maybe she struck a bargain with him. He probably didn't want my company any more than I wanted to take part in a forced conversation. Yet he was standing there looking, I don't know, sincere. And it wasn't like I had anything else to do. So I said sure, and we headed down the hall together.

The kitchen felt different at night without Rita and with only a few ceiling bulbs instead of a flood of natural light. It was cavernous and aloof, if a room can feel that way. I took a stool by the butcher block, hoping I hadn't made a mistake in coming.

"Let's see, what's good in here?" George said with his head in the fridge. "Cheese, oranges, more cheese, pickles. What's this?" He turned around to show me the chilling dough ball in his hands.

"It's *pain d'amandes*. Rita and I made it."

"Let's cook it up," he said.

"B-but—" This was *my* project. My first project with Rita. Not his midnight snack. "It's Rita's dough. She said we were going to bake it in the morning."

"Believe me, she'll be thrilled to know I used it, especially when she finds out you taught me how."

"But I don't *know* how."

"So we'll fudge."

I was about to protest but thought better of it. "Fine," I said. "But if we burn the kitchen down, it's on your head."

"I'm not worried." He breezily set the dough on the island and began banging cupboards open and shut in search of a baking sheet. When he found a tin he liked, he smeared it with butter, then dug into the precious dough with his fingers. He plopped a hunk onto the sheet, and then another and another, not pausing until the tin was plastered with lopsided blobs of my former *pain d'amandes* dough. Rita's dough. Our dough.

"So what do you think?" he said when the demolition was finished. "350, 375?"

"350 what?" I asked weakly.

"Degrees," he laughed. "Never mind, I'll try 450. They'll cook faster." He shoved the pan into the oven and took the stool next to mine. "So," he said, running his fingers along the butcher block, "did Rita tell you the legend of the almonds?"

"No. I mean, not yet. She didn't tell me yet."

"Then I guess I'll have to tell you," he said, scooting his stool a little closer, close enough that I could see the scar in his eyebrow from the long ago crawlspace fall. "It's like this. Once upon a time, a knight had to leave his damsel. He didn't want to—they were in love—but there was a dragon to fight. He promised to return as soon as he could, and she believed him."

George paused to clear his throat, and when he continued, his voice was different, letting slip a trace of—could it be?—warmth, maybe even a hint of shyness. "The knight didn't come home that night. Or the next night or the next. Every day the maiden stood on the fortress wall scanning the horizon for him, and every night she went to bed alone. She waited for years until she finally died of a broken heart."

George had one hand on the island and the other on his crossed leg. He seemed to have a hard time looking straight at me. I smelled Old Spice on him—Old Spice and cookie dough and a trace of mint toothpaste.

"The gods felt sorry for her though, and turned her into an almond tree," he said. "When the knight finally returned with the head of the dragon on his javelin, he was inconsolable when he learned he'd lost his true love. He hugged the almond tree to hide his tears, and when he did, an amazing thing happened. The tree burst into bloom, to show that death hadn't conquered her love for him." George swallowed. "And that is the legend of the almond."

"That's, that's a good story," I stumbled.

"If you believe in that stuff."

"What stuff? Love? Hope? Almonds?"

"You know, all that stuff about—oh, I don't know." Then to make sure I wouldn't press him, he declared that the cookies must be ready. Before I could get another word out, he was off his stool and squinting through the oven window. "Here we go," he said, pulling a bright red mitt onto each hand. "Let's see what we got."

I braced for disappointment, for burnt odors and bitterness and maybe some smoke. But when he opened the oven door, a tidal wave of exquisite smells rushed out. Apparently, Rita's magic was hearty, able to survive even George's mishandling. He carried the pan to the island and gingerly set the biggest, nuttiest cookie in front of me.

I reached for it hungrily, but George tapped my hand. "It's hot," he warned, and I couldn't help but notice how strange his touch felt to my skin—both warm and cold, kind and taunting, placid and disturbing.

When the steam let up and I sank my teeth into the crunchy spicy cookie, I was transported back to Somerville and Mrs. Toussaint's kitchen. Mrs. Toussaint was the old Haitian lady who lived upstairs from us in one of our walk-ups. I was only four, too young for school, and she was lonesome, so she took care of me while Mom worked. Mrs. Toussaint had a Creole accent that I loved, and she called me her *makàk*, her monkey. Every day she baked something different out of the same bunch of ingredients—flour, sugar, butter, eggs—and then we ate it for lunch and supper. Those felt like the good old days, me and Mrs. T., staving off sadness in the kitchen. I hope she enjoyed those times as much as I did, because I can't imagine that my mother paid her much, if anything.

"Mmm," George munched, his eyes at half-mast, his mouth dotted with crumbs. He licked the specks off his lips and then gave his glistening fingers the same treatment. "Good, huh?"

"I've gotta admit it. You fudged good."

He smiled a sticky smile.

Then I asked him something I'd been puzzling over all day. "Hey George, what's with the spy wear?"

He looked at me like I had food all over my face.

"Your sweatshirt." I pointed to the CIA lettering. "You an agent or something?"

He peered at his chest and broke out in a belly laugh. "This CIA isn't for Central Intelligence Agency. It's for the Culinary Institute of America. I'm a second year chef student."

"You're a chef?" I accused, flabbergasted. "You had me thinking you didn't know your way around a kitchen, and you're really a chef?"

He stood up casually and got a bottle of milk from the fridge. "I didn't 'have you' thinking anything. All I said was I didn't know what temperature to bake the cookies at." He sat back down and took a long drink from the bottle. "You didn't tell me your life story either. High school?"

Suddenly I felt too young, or maybe too unaccomplished. I didn't want to be just a high school junior. There was more to me than that...wasn't there? "Uh, yeah," I confessed.

"You don't sound too enthusiastic."

"Well, you know how high school can be."

"Isn't there anything you like about it? One class, one person, one club?"

"I guess I like my English class this term—creative writing.

We're doing short stories right now. I've got one due right after the break."

"Cool." He pushed his stool back and stretched out his legs, like he was just settling in. "Tell me about your story." In the dim light of the night kitchen, both of George's eyes shone green.

"Not yet," I said, hoping he'd find my answer mysterious, not dismissive. The thing is, for all I knew, my story was a load of gunk, and I didn't want him to be the one to confirm it.

"At least tell me the title," he coaxed.

I took the bottle from him and twirled it around. "I guess I can give you that much." I took a sip of the milk—whole milk, heavy and sweet and creamy. "It's 'The Purple Agony.' It's a murder mystery."

"'The Purple Agony,'" he said slowly, like he was tasting the words. "Intriguing. So, are you writing this story on your jeans?"

I looked down at my pants, embarrassed. I'm so used to seeing my hen-scratched quotes on the denim, I don't really see them anymore. "No, no. It's just, when I hear or read a phrase I like, I write it down on the nearest surface. Guess I should start carrying a notebook in my pocket."

He laughed again and then neither of us spoke for a moment. To break the silence, I asked him if the CIA was here on the island. Sounding a little offended, he said Islemorow would sink if something the size of the CIA landed on it. "The Institute is in New York. Hyde Park. It's a real college. Dorms and everything. I mean—sorry. It's just that some people think I'm learning how to assemble Big Macs down there."

"You know what?" I said. "There's an actual Dunkin Donuts University near Boston. My mom used to assistant manage a D.D. in Waltham, and she got sent to the university once to learn, I don't know, how to get the cream inside the éclairs or something." I was expecting him to be amused, but the mere mention of my mother seemed to derail him. He looked baffled, as if he'd lost complete track of the conversation. In desperation, I heard myself ask, "Um, so how'd you get into cooking, anyway? Rita, I bet."

The change of subject—or maybe the reference to Rita—roused George from his stupor. "She was a great teacher. Still is."

"You two are close then."

He took the bottle back from me and stared deep into the milk. "Yeah. She was around more than my mom growing up, you know? Ma was always off trying to start some new business. I used to hang out here in the kitchen just for something to do. The cooking, it kind of rubbed off on me by accident. But it's a good fit, just the same."

To my chagrin, another silence filled the short distance between us. I wondered what George was thinking. I wondered if he was wondering what I was thinking. And then I started babbling. "Well, I guess I should get some sleep now." I stood up, talking fast. "So I can, you know, get some work done tomorrow. Besides, you're probably exhausted after your headache. I hope Rita doesn't mind that we did this. Wait, we'd better do some cleaning up, and—"

"Penny." He didn't seem nearly as tense as I suddenly was. "It's okay. I just had a nap. I'll clean up. You go to bed."

"No, I helped make the mess."

He got up and pointed sternly toward the door. "Go to bed. You need to be rested for our outing tomorrow morning."

"What outing?"

"I don't know yet, but I'll think of something."

This evoked several responses in me. I was (a) delighted at the thought of getting out of the inn for a while, (b) curious about this so-called outing, (c) wary about what state of mind the mood-swinging George would be in come morning, and (d) confused. Hopefully, a decent night's sleep would give me some clarity—*and* help me keep my wits about me tomorrow.

"Go on," he said. "You're tired."

Now that he mentioned it, I was. "If you're sure."

"I'm positive."

"Good night then. See you in the morning."

"Night."

I left the kitchen without looking back at him, wondering if he was watching me go. No matter. It didn't matter. I headed straight upstairs. Why had George shared the fairy tale about love and longing though and sat so close to me when he told it? What did he mean by *outing*? I pondered these delicious questions while I walked down the hall, under the chandelier and past the watercolors. It wasn't until I was almost at my room that I noticed Blue standing outside my door with an armful of logs.

I can believe anything, provided that it is quite incredible.
—*Oscar Wilde*

"Hey," I said.

"I thought you might like a fire," Blue said. "It's a cold one tonight."

"Wow, thanks." Talk about service.

I let us in, and Blue unloaded the wood into the hearth. He crumpled up some newspaper pages he'd brought along and tossed them on top of the logs. Then he lit a match and touched it to the paper, which blackened and curled with the heat.

"This'll give you a nice light," he said, jostling the logs with a poker. As the flames caught, they threw a warm color onto his cheeks, like apricots or maybe mangoes. "There's nothing like a fire, is there? Here, let me teach you how to stoke it, in case it needs some help later."

"Okay, show me the trick," I said, joining him by the hearth.

"No trick. You just need to give the flames some air. Want to give it a try?"

I took the poker and wiggled it against the bottom log. Several orange and blue flames plumed around it with a gleeful pop, like school kids being let out for recess. I must have nudged too hard though, because one of the logs tumbled off the pile, hitting the stone hearth and rolling toward us.

"Blue!" I gasped, reaching instinctively for his shoulder.

The Black Butterfly

But instead of gripping his shoulder, my hand went
right
    through
        him.

Right through him, as if he weren't even there. I was
supposed to be feeling muscle, skin and bone pressing through
his flannel shirt. My hand was supposed to be confirming what
my eyes told me was true. People were supposed to be solid
things that pushed back against your touch. Why wasn't Blue
cooperating with the simple rules of the universe?

He grabbed the poker from me and took care of the log
while I stood catatonic at his side. All I could do was gape at
him, my hand, and back at him, trying to convince myself that
nothing had just happened, that I'd simply aimed my hand
wrong and missed his shoulder. But no, I knew I wasn't that
much of a spaz. I felt winded. Nauseous. Wobbly.

"I frightened you," he said softly. "I'm sorry, Penny. I, I
just can't believe you can see me."

With my heart thrashing my chest, I asked, "Are you saying
most people can't?"

"You're the first."

"My God." I felt like I was going to pass out, like all the
blood was leaving my head and running for its life. My knees
started to buckle.

"We better get you off your feet."

I dropped onto the loveseat and put my head between my
knees. My fight or flight instinct couldn't make up its mind. I
just sat there in a puddle of useless adrenaline. "Who, what are
you? Why are you even here?"

"I died here. A century ago."

I sat up slowly, trying to comprehend what he was telling me. "So then, you really are a...?" I couldn't say the word. "How...?"

"I was part of a fishing crew," he said, sitting next to me. "We trolled up and down the Eastern seaboard catching herring. One summer night, we moored at Islemorow on our way to Nova Scotia. I ended up taking my supper right here, at the place that used to stand here. There was a fire, and I didn't get out in time."

But he looked so damned real, so alive, so here and now. Could it be true, what he was saying? Did I really just put my hand through the spirit of a person who died a hundred years ago? It made no sense, and yet...

"Penny?"

"Huh? Oh, sorry. I mean, God, I'm so sorry. How old were you?"

"Twenty-one."

Yes, he looked twenty-one. So young to die. So pointless. I thought of *Arson for Hire*, a gruesome novel that described how a body burns in a fire. What that book didn't describe was how it felt to burn alive. How excruciating was the pain Blue endured? Did he see his eyes melt? Hear his own voice screaming? Feel his brain boil?

Suddenly, I couldn't get enough oxygen into my lungs. "Hold on for a second," I panted, waiting either to faint, throw up, or feel better. When the black spots in front of me disappeared, I said, "I'll just wait right here until I wake up."

"You think you're dreaming me?"

I bit my lip.

"Because there's more, Penny. I want to tell you the rest, but not if it's going to make you sick."

I didn't say anything for a long time. I wanted to hear his story, but at the same time, I didn't. I didn't want to believe this was happening. I didn't want to believe my crazy mother was right.

"Tell me," I finally said.

He narrowed his eyes and gazed at me doubtfully.

"Really, Blue, I want to know."

"All right. The thing about the fire, the truth is, I started it. I'm the one who burned down the Legacy Hotel and Resort."

Oh, God. I didn't just have a ghost on my hands, I had the ghost of a pyromaniac. Or maybe worse—maybe he was a psychopath or criminally insane. I looked at the fire roaring in the hearth. I started to stand up but felt woozy all over again and had to stay put. *Humor him, Penny. Humor him until you can get up and run the hell out of here.* "W-well, you, um, must have had some reason for setting the fire."

He looked at me in amazement. "I didn't set the fire. It was an accident."

"Ohhhh," I said, too relieved to feel very embarrassed. I sank back into the loveseat cushions. "I just…anyway, how did it happen? I mean, how do you know you're the one?"

"Easy. The fire started in the dining room, and I was the last person in there. Just sitting there enjoying an after-supper cigarette before heading to the parlor to hear the music. Thing is, I had a bad habit of not snuffing out my butts. On the boat, we just threw them overboard, you know? Stupid, stupid carelessness. Cost me my life."

I pulled my hoodie closer. Clutched my elbows. Groaned. "God."

"Sorry you asked?" he said.

"It's not that. It's…is this what happens after you die?" I asked, although I was pretty sure I didn't want to hear the answer. "You linger?"

"Not usually. Most people cross over right away. I chose to stay."

"You *chose* to stay in the place where you were incinerated?"

"Penny, I'm not the only one who died in that fire. A child—a baby—burned too. Because of me. I will not leave this place until I can make up for taking a life. I will not go until I can help someone, really help someone. Do you understand?"

No, I didn't. I didn't understand anything. "So you've spent a hundred years just waiting around for someone to save. Jesus, don't you die of boredom? I mean, sorry, but what do you do with yourself all day?"

"I take walks. Think. Journey sometimes."

"Journey. So you get to travel." That part didn't sound so bad. Less monotonous, anyway.

"Dream journey." He sat cross-legged and closed his eyes, tapping his knees with splayed fingers. "A different kind of traveling. It takes you farther, deeper. My Finnish grandfather taught me—he fancied himself a bit of a shaman." He opened his eyes. "You should come with me sometime."

"God, this is wild." I moved closer and reached a tentative hand toward him. "Is this okay?" He nodded, so I continued, trying to rest my fingertips on his knee. My hand fell straight

The Black Butterfly 71

through to the loveseat below. "You try touching me now, see if it'll work that way."

Blue looked pessimistic, but he did as I asked. First, he put his hand on the top of my head, then play-punched my leg, and finally tried to lift my arm. Nothing worked. I didn't feel a thing.

"Whoa, wait a minute," I said. "How did you carry in those logs or light the match or handle the poker, if you're like this?"

"I don't understand it myself. I'm fine with things that aren't alive. But give me a warm body, and I turn to vapor. I can't even swat a mosquito." He laughed, but it was a heartbroken laugh. "Imagine trying to help someone when you can't pick them up, pull them out, carry them, or even hold their hand. That's part of the reason I've been here so long."

I tried one last time to touch him, but it was no use. That athletic, arrow-straight body was all vapor. I moved back to my side of the loveseat. "You should go," I said.

His face fell. "I've overstayed my welcome." He uncrossed his legs and started to stand.

"No," I said, motioning him to sit back down. "You should go wherever you go when you cross over. You've tried long enough to help someone. You should leave this place."

"I won't."

"What a terrible sentence to serve."

"Until today, the worst part was not knowing when I'd ever have a real person to talk to again. If ever." His eyes were blazing.

I couldn't stop watching him, his hands, his high cheeks, his collarbones sticking out from his shirt. His body looked so solid, so firm and solid, but it wasn't. He really was a ghost.

I was sitting here chatting with a man who died before my grandparents were even born. I started to shiver.

"You're cold," he said. "I'll turn up the heat."

"No, it's not that. It's just so bizarre. Why is it I can see you, and the others can't?"

He cocked his head as if to see me from a different angle. "You have a gift."

"I'm not sure I want it," I blurted. "I mean—I didn't mean it like that."

"It's okay, I get it. I'm not sure I'd want to know me if the tables were turned."

"But…" I wanted to say something, but my words got lost in my spinning head.

"Listen, why don't you sleep on it? I should get going."

"Sleep, after this?"

He stood up.

"You don't have to go," I said, but he was already on his way to the door. "I didn't mean what I said. That was the shock talking."

"Don't worry, I'll come by again—if it's all right." He put his hand on the knob, then paused. "No stalking though, I promise."

He was gone before I realized I hadn't even said good night.

As I suspected, sleep didn't come easily. When it finally did, I still didn't get any rest, just crazy dreams. I was on a sailboat way out in the ocean, with no land in sight. George was on the boat too, but he didn't know me, or maybe he was pretending not to know me. Mom rowed up in a little dinghy, video cameras hanging all over her. When I called out to her, everything changed, and I was sitting on a porch swing, rocking a baby in my arms. A dead baby.

I tried to scream, but no sound came out. Suddenly, it started to pour. The whole porch filled up with rain, and the water washed me all the way back to the ocean, where the sailboat was waiting for me.

I don't remember how the dream ended, but I know I was glad to wake up.

Chapter 4

*The secret of life is to appreciate the pleasure of being
terribly, terribly deceived.*
—Oscar Wilde

Rita was grinding coffee beans when I got to the kitchen late
the next morning. Even though I was a little peeved at her for
standing me up last night, I was grateful to be in a room with
a live, flesh-and-blood person. Don't get me wrong, I liked
Blue. He seemed like a great guy. But Jesus, he was a ghost. He
was everything I denied and everything Mom clung to. He was a
million questions and not enough answers. He was there and he
wasn't there, and he was sledgehammering my version of reality.

"Hi," I said, positioning myself across the island from Rita.

"Good morning." She finished grinding the beans, turned
off the machine, and dumped the grounds into a gold filter
before looking up.

"What happened to you last night?" I asked, hoping to
sound concerned, not accusatory.

"I am sorry?"

"Last night in the study. I thought we were supposed to
meet there after supper. Did I have it wrong?"

Rita plunked the filter into the coffee machine. "But I did
not say I would come."

"Oh," I said, puzzled. "I must have misunderstood."

"I said you should go to the study. I never said I would be there."

"But —" Then it dawned on me. "You told George to go to the study too, didn't you?"

Rita shook her head. "I did not tell George to go. I know he watches the news in the study every night, that is all. Tell me, was it really so bad?" Her vibe was all guileless and apologetic, making it hard to be annoyed.

"Well," I started, but suddenly Vincent was calling Rita from the dining room.

"I must go," she said. "Come back this afternoon. You tell me about last night, and I will teach you how to prepare an artichoke." Sounded like I was getting the short end of that stick. And I didn't even know the study had a TV.

Alone again, I went over to watch the coffee perk. Then, just as I was about to pour myself a stiff mug, a voice behind me said, "You ready?"

I looked up to see George leaning in the doorway, smiling and apparently relaxed. *Thank God*. I'd already started to wonder (slash worry) where he was this morning—not just where he was in the house, but where he was in his head. Was he going to be Grumpy or Happy today, or would he be switching back and forth? Was he going to like me, maybe even like me "that way," or was he going to resent my very existence? From the looks of him now, it seemed like Nice George had come out to play. Maybe he really did just have a lousy headache yesterday. And the day before. Maybe there was hope.

"Ready for what?" I asked as nonchalantly as I could.

"Early lunch. Let's go out."

"The Grindle Point Shop?"

"You've been then?" He sounded disappointed.

"No, I just saw the sign on the way in. I haven't been out of the house since I got here."

"C'mon then, grab your coat. We'll take the van."

Was he asking me out on a date? All I could do was study him and hope the answer was printed on his face. What should I say?

"Say yes," he said. I ran upstairs to retrieve my jacket and mittens.

As I hurried down the hall on my way back to George, the door to the Tiger Lily room opened, and a girl emerged—the same girl I'd seen in the parlor when I first arrived at the inn. She was barefoot this time, her hair in a ponytail, and she was staring, not just looking, at me.

I diverted my eyes, thinking I'd just walk past her and be on my way. No such luck. She planted herself in the middle of the hallway and raised a hand to stop me.

Now what? I stopped a few feet away from her. "Hello?" I said uneasily.

"Listen here," she said, her voice wispy and low. "I'm going to say this one time: stay away from Blue. Do you hear me? Stay away from him if you know what's good for you."

Hold everything. This chick knew Blue? She could see him? But I thought I was the first one. The only one.

She took a step closer. "Did you hear me?"

I blinked. That was all I could muster.

Tipping her head to one side, she looked me over the way you'd inspect a used car on the sales lot. "Not the prettiest shell on the beach, are you?" she said. "Not much style either." Her eyes drifted from my sweatshirt to my ratty jeans to my scuffed clogs. Then she raised a slender finger and poked me in the chest, only I didn't feel a thing. She was vapor.

"Oh," I said dumbly. Obviously, Blue left out part of the story when he told me about himself. Was this girl Blue's family? Girlfriend? Had they known each other in life, or only since death? Why didn't Blue want me to know about her? And what was she so suspicious about?

"Did you hear me?" she demanded.

"What? What do you want from me?"

"Penny," came George's voice from the bottom of the stairs. "You talking to yourself? C'mon, I'm starving."

"I told you what I want from you," she said. "I want you to keep away from Blue." With that, she turned around and disappeared into the Tiger Lily room.

"On my way," I called down, throwing on my jacket and my Normal Face. I'd have to save the falling to pieces for later, alone. Right now, I had George waiting for me. I just hoped my Mask of Composure would fool him.

🦋

He'd make a lovely corpse.
—Charles Dickens, Martin Chuzzlewit

George opened the van door for me to get in—did that make it a date? I didn't know, but I resolved to just enjoy myself. So what if George baffled me—it was kind of fun this way. And double so what if Ghost Girl had freaked me out? At this point, I couldn't really remember what she'd even said or done. She was like a faded memory that couldn't find its way to the surface...which was strange, since the encounter had just happened. In the end, I decided not to stress about something I couldn't recollect.

"I get to sit in front this time?" I asked coyly as I hopped in.

"Your status has been elevated."

Elevated to what? Pal, potential hookup, possible love interest? *Slow down, cowgirl, you're getting way ahead of yourself. Again.* We pulled out of the driveway and bumped along the snowy, barren road.

"There's the bakery," he said, pointing to a lean-to off of someone's bungalow. "And that," he nodded toward a small brick building set back from the road, "that was my school, K-12. See the footbridge next to it? According to legend, if a boy and a girl cross paths on that bridge when no one else is around, they have to kiss."

"The only legend at my school is its bad food," I said. *Stupid, stupid.* George was talking kissing, and I came back with cafeteria. Fortunately, he thought this was funny, and I got to see those dimples pop when he laughed.

"How big was your graduating class?" I asked.

He smirked. "That's what my CIA friends ask when they find out I was salutatorian. They want to know if that put me in the top half or the bottom half."

"Well?"

"There were fourteen of us that year," he said, turning into the parking lot at our destination. "Practically a record. We had the Bucolla triplets and the Winooski twins to thank for that."

What a different world he grew up in. In Boston, I've never had a classroom, much less a whole grade, with less than 25 kids, which is probably for the best—it's easier to hide yourself in a crowd, easier to avoid being noticed or being asked questions about where you live. I'd have died living on Islemorow. Visiting, however, was taking a turn for the better at the moment.

The Grindle Point Shop was a book nook, gift store, diner and takeout stand all rolled into one. It had a barn feel to it— lots of exposed wood, a high sloping ceiling, open layout, a grab bag of smells. Blinking holiday lights looped around the walls like the scalloped edges of a piecrust. "Sleigh Ride" boomed from a hidden stereo. A wood stove was working double time in the corner, and after the walk from the parking lot, the blast of warm air felt delicious.

We hit a typical crowd today, George informed me as we walked toward the eating area. Xandros, the island's only resident attorney, was the one drinking coffee at the counter and taking off his helmet. "He actually has snow tires on his bike. And over there by the magazines," he said, touching my arm, "that's Thaddeus. He runs a combination hardware/Bible store down the road. Something about Jesus being a carpenter."

Maybe I was imagining things, but it didn't feel like a simple I-want-to-direct-your-attention-to-this-corner-of-the-room tap of his hand on my arm. It was a more deliberate touch, released with a barely there stroke of his fingertips. I glanced up at him, and he smiled casually back, revealing nothing, the male Mona Lisa.

"Who's the bald guy behind the cash register?" I asked.

"That's Buddy, he owns the place. The old lady bending his ear is Mrs. Walker the Talker. No one knows what she looks like with her mouth closed. Here, I'll save him. Hey, Buddy," he called across the room. "Over here."

Buddy, a tall man with a baby-smooth complexion, rushed over to greet us. "Look who's back in town," he grinned, shaking George's hand in vigorous thanks for the out.

"Buddy, this is my friend Penny. She's staying with us for a couple of weeks. First time at the inn."

"Really?" His eyes widened. "You're in for a treat, Penny. Did George tell you Dan Shwam of the Catskill Cougars once sailed here all the way from Bar Harbor just to eat supper at the Black Butterfly? Or that Chip Hutchins—y'know, from the Bangor Lumberjacks— stayed at the inn for a weekend after the big one in Quebec?"

"I...no," I said, wondering if these were household names that had somehow escaped my awareness.

"That's right, and José Garcia—"

"Buddy's all about baseball," George explained. "He wouldn't notice if the Pope walked in, but give him a ball player no one's ever heard of, and he's all over it. So Buddy, how's that skiff you were building last time we talked?"

Boats seemed to excite Buddy almost as much as athlete sightings. I listened politely for a few minutes and then excused myself to the book nook. This seemed like as good a time as any to explore the place.

I circled the three book carousels that stood between the postcard rack and the jukebox, wondering if anything would draw my attention. The first carousel was crammed with magazines of either the sportsman or handyman sort—not my bag. The second carousel, larger and harder to turn, carried novelty books: *Compendium of Ocean Meditations*, *Angling: A Pop-Up Book for the Rod and Line Enthusiast*, *Ten-Minute Brain Teasers*—not my type either. The last carousel, marked clearance, was my only hope. My eyes went straight to a small hardcover book near the bottom. It had a black spine that, intriguingly, had no title on it. I squatted down and pulled it out.

Lacking the typical glossy paper flap, the woven cover felt rough in my hands, as if it had been hand sewn by a cobbler instead of whizbanged together by a high-speed press. The front was a solid shade of ice blue, the color of winter or my birthstone or forget-me-nots. Across the top, in calligraphy style, it called itself *Facts and Fancies about Islemorow*. Below that, in smaller but equally fancy type, it added *By One of the Very Oldest Cottagers*. I had to turn to the copyright page to learn the name of the old cottager: Alda M. Eldenberry, who self-published the book in 2005 under the business name Berry Press.

The book was heavy for its slender size, as if the words inside were substantial enough to add weight to the silver-rimmed pages. There were five chapters:

1) Cabbages and Kings: Founding Fathers

2) Fire and Ice: Nature on the Island

3) Sticks and Stones: Local Architecture

4) Bed Knobs and Broomsticks: Islemorow During the World Wars

5) Sweet and Sour: Automobiles, Motorboats and Other Progress

Opposite the table of contents, an aerial photo offered
a bird's eye view of the island. I tried to find the inn, and I
thought I picked it out, but I wasn't sure. I wasn't even sure
which side of the pickle-shaped, fifteen square-mile island the
inn sat on. And since the photo was all beachfront and forest
and dot-sized roofs, it wasn't a simple task for someone who
has trouble finding North on a map.

Alda M. Eldenberry offered this counsel in the photo caption:
"Islemorow hasn't changed much since the early days, and that's
just fine to this old cottager's way of thinking. There's no better
place on earth if you know how to make your own fun, if you adore
the simple rhythm of the tide, and if you don't mind a quirky
neighbor or two. But if you prefer movie theaters, cafés and
conventional personalities, you may wish to stay on the mainland."

Curious about the Black Butterfly's past, I turned to the
Sticks and Stones chapter. On the first page was an ink drawing
of the inn, its front door open in a welcoming gesture. "A lavish
20-room resort called the Legacy once stood on the site of the
Black Butterfly," Alda wrote. "Built to house wealthy Harvard
boys on their summer holidays, the Legacy burned down in
1910. Only the earthen-floor basement, part of one staircase,
the old chain-pull toilets, and a metal safe survived."

The Legacy. The long ago fire. Blue. My hands began to
shake. I had to own Mrs. Eldenberry's work, even though it
suddenly frightened me just to hold it.

I read on: "Five years after the fatal fire, the esteemed
painter Cleo Easton bought the land and built a home on the
site. Her family transformed it into the Black Butterfly Inn
after her death in 1954 and sold it to Wilson Henion in 1974."

There was no price marked anywhere on the book. That probably meant it was expensive, even at clearance price. Still, I wanted it. I spotted Buddy feeding the wood stove and hurried over to him.

"Find something interesting?" Buddy asked, closing the stove door.

"Yes," I said, trying not to sound overly eager. "This book about the island looks like a good read. How much is it?"

He extended his hand, and I gave him the book. "*Facts and Fancies*," he said. "I didn't realize we still had any copies."

"It was the only one left."

He turned the book over a couple of times, looking puzzled. "Doesn't seem to be marked, does it? Hardcovers usually start at twenty though."

That wasn't going to work. Then I remembered. "It was in clearance. What does that do to the price?"

"In that case, we knock off a couple of bucks, just to try to move it out of here. If that doesn't work, we switch it back up to full price and start all over." He started to laugh but must have seen my face fall, because he immediately added, "You know what? This thing looks like it's been kicking around forever. Why don't we call it a loan? Take it to the inn with you, and try to get it back to me before you go. If you remember."

"Really?" I said hopefully.

"Hey, any friend of the Henions is a friend of mine. Enjoy."

"Thanks, Buddy." I turned to go, then added over my shoulder, "I'll take good care of it."

When I looked for George to tell him about my find, I spotted him standing near the take-out counter, deep in conversation with someone. Remembering that Bubbles had some of her work here, I wandered over to the jewelry display.

Bubbles' few pieces were easy to spot with their signature glass chips and computer entrails. There was a ring that was kind of pretty if you didn't mind it covering the knuckles of two fingers, and a bunch of bangles in assorted metallic colors. My favorite item was a set of seemingly mismatched earrings. One earring was the question mark from a keyboard. The other was a blue circle of glass with the Chinese symbol for serenity painted on it—sort of a yin and yang thing, I guessed.

After a few minutes, a voice behind me said, "I see you have an appreciation for great art, Miss." It was George.

"Do you know absolutely everyone on the island?"

"This time of year I do. It's all townies, no tourists. C'mon, let's sit. I ordered us some soup."

We took a little corner table, white Formica with red chairs, next to one of the shop's few windows. When we each rested a hand on the table, our fingertips practically touched. God, I love hands. They're so much of how you experience the world. In biology last year, we learned that the human hand has 1,300 nerve endings per square inch. So when two hands touch each other, well, you can do the math. As for me, I didn't need actual contact to set all those thousands of nerves ablaze.

"See anything interesting in the shop?" George asked.

Oh, right, we were supposed to talk to each other, not just sit here while I shamelessly lusted after him. I pulled myself together. "Look what Buddy let me borrow," I said, pulling the book out from under my arm and passing it to him.

"*Facts and Fancies about Islemorow,*" he read. "Looks familiar. I think we have a copy of it at the inn."

"Really? Maybe I should return this one to Buddy then."

"Don't bother. Even if we do have it, who knows where it is?" I put the book back into my purse. "Have you ever read it?"

He scratched the back of his head. "Hmmm. Does it have a drawing of the inn?"

"That's right. A drawing and a little history."

"I think I've glanced through the pictures." Then his attention shifted. "Look over there," he said, pointing out the window. "See that lady across the street, the one in the red coat, shoveling snow off her car?"

I turned to see a woman hardly as tall as her shovel, who looked old enough to give Alda M. Eldenberry a run for her money as one of the very oldest cottagers.

"That's Miss McQuiggan," he said. "She was my teacher for three years in elementary school—she was about 90 back then." We watched as she loaded her shovel into her trunk and took off in a burst of fumes. "I think she's gotten younger as I've gotten older."

I spent a minute watching the snowy little world go by: a man in an Elmer Fudd hunting cap, a child bundled up like a mummy, a pickup truck with a snowmobile in tow. Across the road was Cliff's General Market, which, according to the handwritten sign on the door, also housed the post office. Next door to Cliff's stood a shack with a snowed-over barber's pole in front. After that was Suzy's Boating Supplies, clearly closed up for the winter. And then there was nothing, nothing but snow and scrub, until the road disappeared around a bend. If I could just take this view and shake it, I'd have the perfect snow globe souvenir of the island.

"When I was a little kid," he said, "I used to love sitting at this window. I'd press my nose right up against the glass and see if I could pick out the people who must be my parents."

Wait a minute, was he saying...?

"I'm adopted," he said. "That's why Ma and I don't look anything alike. Or hadn't you noticed?" This was a rhetorical question. Where Bubbles was thickset and fair, George was—there's no other way to put it—tall, dark and handsome.

"I take it you never found them," I said.

"Nope." He absently touched his eyebrow scar. "And I probably never will. It was a closed adoption."

"I'm sorry," I said. "I mean, not that you're adopted—Bubbles is great. It's just that, you know..." I had no idea what I was saying. "Sorry. I'm sorry."

"No need," he said cheerfully. "Besides, it's not over yet, right?"

"Right," I said, even though it sounded to me like George's chances of meeting his parents were about as good as my chances of meeting The Donor.

Then our waiter arrived, and the topic was dropped. Buddy was carrying two styrofoam bowls of soup and two paper cups of tea. Apparently, it was supposed to be French onion soup, but it was more like beef bouillon with a slice of Wonder bread and a glob of Velveeta cheese floating on top. "This is our specialité du maison," he said, setting the bowls down in front of us.

"Looks great," I lied. "Thank you."

"Oh, I forgot your water. Be right back, unless I forget." He winked at me and turned to the table behind us.

George motioned me to start, so I took a spoonful. It tasted like it looked. Trying not to grimace, I forced it down and set the spoon back on the table.

"That bad?" George asked.

"I guess Rita's got me spoiled. But you go ahead."

He dipped his spoon between the droopy bread and the soggy onions and lifted it to his lips. The broth got into his mouth okay, but the Cheez Whiz didn't want to come off his spoon, so he bit it off instead. "Not so awful," he said, still chewing the cheese, "as long as you don't breathe through your nose...hold on, saved by the bell."

He took his cell phone out of his back pocket. "Hello...hey, Smitty, what's up?...I didn't see it...yeah, that's weird...I'll take a look when I get home...got it. See ya." He clicked off. "Mike Smitty—the repairman—he misplaced his cordless saw. Thinks the last place he had it was the inn, so he wants me to look around."

Odd. I mean, how do you misplace something the size and weight of a power tool?

"But enough about Smitty and soup and me," he said. "Will you tell me about 'The Purple Agony' now?"

He remembered the title of my short story! I felt embarrassed, shy, flattered. If he was interested in my story, did that mean he was interested in me?

"Please?" George asked oh so sweetly. He dropped his spoon and leaned toward me, chin on hand.

"Okay, all right." I cleared my throat. "'The Purple Agony'

is the story of a prizewinning photojournalist. This guy is always in the right place at the right time—you know, just when disaster strikes, he's there to snap the picture. Well, late one Christmas Eve, he finds the body of a homeless woman on a deserted road, victim of a hit and run. She's wearing flip-flops even though it's freezing out, and she's clutching a dahlia, the symbol of dignity that she just received at midnight mass. He snaps the photo, and it appears on front pages nationwide on Christmas Day."

George nodded attentively.

"Only, down at the soup kitchen, they knew this woman. They say she never went to church, never went out that late, never wore flip-flops. Turns out she'd collapsed on the street sometime earlier that night, and when the photographer happened to cruise by, he purposefully ran her over, then put the flower in her hand and exchanged her boots for flip-flops before taking the picture. P.S., he's been staging fires and accidents for years. This is just the first time he got caught."

I took a gulp of air and waited for George's reaction. He gazed at me intently, somberly. "Say something," I said when I couldn't stand it any longer.

"Why's it called 'The Purple Agony'?"

"Because of the purple camera flash. That purple dot you see after a camera flashes in your face."

He narrowed his eyes. "It's blue."

"What?"

"The dot. It's blue."

I grabbed the napkin off my lap and squashed it into a tight ball. "Maybe I'll change it to 'The Blue Agony,' or 'The Cobalt Agony,' or maybe 'The Periwinkle Bordering on Indigo Agony.'"

"Stop," he laughed, sitting back. "I like it, truly. A real page turner. I can't wait to see the movie."

"It's not just a crime thriller," I said, hearing the edge in my voice. "It's supposed to make you think. Like, maybe this guy simply has no regard for human life. But maybe it's more complicated than that. Maybe in his personal hell, he's convinced himself he's making art."

George's eyebrows rose. "Well, which is it?"

"Both, sort of. Like this soup here. It's evil, but it's just trying to do its job."

"Well then," he pinned his eyes on mine, "maybe the next meal we share should be homemade. By someone who knows something about cooking."

My cheeks flamed. No male has ever cooked for me. In fact, short of Rita and old Mrs. Toussaint, I couldn't think of *anyone* who'd ever cooked for me. And now this! George wanted to use those beautiful hands and all their thousands of nerve endings to create a meal for me.

As I racked my brain for something to say back, something alluring or at least playful, I noticed that George was letting his eyes drift dreamily around the room. Was he pondering what he would make for me—brunch or an indoor picnic lunch or a late-night supper for two? Was he envisioning the before, the during, and especially the after? *Dream on, George, dream on. I'll fantasize too, and later we can compare notes.*

Then I realized something: George's room gazing wasn't idle. No, there was definitely a purpose to it. He was peering over my shoulder the same way Chad Laramy had done back at the Logan terminal: eagerly. I fought the urge to look behind me. When George broke into a massive smile, I finally turned around to see if Buddy was bringing us banana splits on the house or something.

A pretty girl in a red leather jacket, jeans and high-heeled boots was walking toward us. George jumped up and met her before she made it to our table. They fell into a tight hug. "Iris, you're here!" George rejoiced.

"I thought I was going to miss you," she cooed. Spotting me, she added, "Is this a bad time? Because I could—"

"No, no, this is perfect," he reveled, tightening his arm around her waist and leading her to the table. "Here, sit down. Iris, this is Penny. Penny, this is my old friend Iris."

Gentle reader, I'm here to tell you that Iris wasn't old, and she obviously wasn't just a friend either.

"Good to meet you, Patty."

"It's Penny," I said.

"Penny? Sorry, it must be these earmuffs." She took off the muffs and flipped her sleek black hair over her shoulder. "There, much better."

George pulled over a chair from the next table and motioned Iris to sit next to him.

"You look terrific, sweetie," she said. "Fill me in."

They leaned in until their noses were almost touching. They looked like one person bent toward a mirror, admiring the reflection. It dawned on me then that maybe Iris was the one who'd given George his crescent moon pendant. How could I have been so stupid? How had I ever dared to think that George was attracted to me? God, I'd actually thought this was a date. That he was intrigued by my short story because he was intrigued by me. That he had romantic designs when he offered to cook for me. I'm such an idiot.

I pushed my chair back a few inches. It squeaked against the floor, but they didn't notice. "Powder room," I said, standing up.

By the time I made it to the bathroom, tears were spattering my cheeks. This was ridiculous. It wasn't like George was my boyfriend. I'd only known him for a couple of days, for God's sake. What was there to be so unhinged over? In a week and a half, I'd be done with this hellhole anyway, and I could return to my reclusive outcast existence in Cambridge. Who needed this crap?

I let myself cry for a minute. As I splashed cold water on my face, Mrs. Walker the Talker came in, so I quickly blew my nose and left. There was no way I was going to let George and Iris see me this way, so I bolted to the book nook.

I had to force myself not to gawk at the lovebirds. I was dying to know if they were touching hands, making plans, making googly eyes at each other. Instead, I read *Field and Stream* and *Woodworking* magazines, counted the books, eavesdropped on Xandros the lawyer and Thaddeus the hardware man. When I was positive the tears were in check, I considered going back to the table, but what was the point? I couldn't compete with someone like Iris. Besides, I didn't have the guts to stake my claim. Not that I *had* a rightful claim, but even if I did, the I-adore-you-Iris look on George's face was all I needed to stop me in my tracks.

Thirty agonizing minutes passed. Then George was standing beside me, holding my purse, which I'd left on my chair. "You okay?" he asked.

"Um, yeah—sorry," I said, taking my purse and feeling my cheeks burn. "I felt a little queasy all of a sudden, and I didn't want to go back near the food."

"The deadly French onion soup, huh? Let me get you home. You feel like you can make it to the car?"

"Uh huh." I walked quickly to the door, and he had to jog a few steps to catch up.

As we crunched along the snow-packed parking lot, he slipped his arm around mine, but I pretended to need to cough and pulled my arm away. When we got to the van, he opened the door for me, and I fell into my seat, avoiding his eyes.

"Is…anything else the matter?" he asked.

"No, nothing's wrong. I'll be fine." The truth, of course, was that something was very wrong—with me. Why else would George have no interest in me? Apparently, I wasn't that kind of girl. I wasn't girlfriend material.

He stood there with his hand on the open door. The wind picked up, and it lifted the hair off of his face. His eyes reflected something, only I couldn't tell whether it was concern or annoyance. "You sure?" he asked.

"Positive. Come on, let's go. I'm getting cold."

He shut my door and ran around to his side. We drove out of the parking lot and onto the road.

"So," I said, trying to sound nonchalant, "is Iris an islander?"

"We grew up together."

Wonderful—she had history *and* looks on me. "You stay in touch, that's nice."

"Yeah, over the holidays and the summers. We're pretty close."

"It seemed that way." Ouch, did that come out snide?

He looked at me curiously. "Anyway, she's leaving town before Christmas for a family reunion, so I'm glad I bumped into her today."

I faked a groan and leaned my head back on the headrest. "I'm just gonna close my eyes for a minute."

"Penny," he said, his voice insistent now, maybe even a little sharp. "What's going on?"

That's exactly what I wanted to know. I said nothing.

"Is this really about one spoonful of half-assed soup? Or…"

I groaned again, clutching my belly this time, and we drove the rest of the way to the inn without talking.

🦋

All hope abandon, ye who enter here!
—*Dante,* THE DIVINE COMEDY

In the time we were gone, Vincent had made an enormous Christmas tree materialize in the parlor corner, ready for decorating, and now he was outside hanging wreaths on the doors and windows. The tree was tall and fat, a gorgeous shade of navy green, and Bubbles was draped on a chair nearby, surveying box after box of sparkly ornaments. If I'd been in a good or even a tolerable mood, I'd have thought it a cozy scene, but I wasn't.

"There you are," sang Bubbles as we tramped into the parlor. "It's time for my favorite holiday tradition. Actually, it's *past* time—I've been waiting for you."

"Sorry," said George. "We...I ran into Iris."

At the sound of this name, Bubbles sat up. "She's home? How is the dear?"

Make your exit now, I told myself. *Don't give George the satisfaction of knowing you're invested in his answer. Invested? Try dying to know.* But my feet were concrete.

"She's great," George said, glancing sideways at me. "I hope it's okay—I invited her to trim the tree with us."

"Lovely," Bubbles clucked. "The more the merrier. It's a party, after all."

"Excuse me," I said, but before I could decide whether to head to my room or the kitchen, Bubbles was making her pitch.

"Penny," she said, looking aghast, "surely you'll join us. We'll hang decorations, sip Rita's famous mulled cider, sing along to Burl Ives. Look, look here." She pulled some glass snowflakes out of their tissue paper wrapping. "These are my latest additions. Aren't they exquisite? And isn't this tree the most enchanting thing you've ever laid eyes on?"

Mom and I have one of those fake white trees, the tabletop edition, which we trim with a few pinecones, plain and simple (except for that one year when we also strung up the doughnut holes Gigi brought us. The cockroaches put an end to that idea the very next morning). Mom and I might be setting up our little tree right now, if we were at home where we belonged.

"Thanks so much, Bubbles," I said, "but I'm nursing a doozy of a headache right now." Damn! I'd told George it was my belly, and now I was claiming it was my head. How transparent could I be? "You go ahead without me."

"Oh, you poor thing," she said, wilting back into her chair.

The Black Butterfly 95

"George shouldn't have dragged you out in the cold with only that bit of a jacket on. Can I get you some Echinacea? It always works for what ails us."

"No, I'll be fine, really. I just need…I think a hot cup of coffee is what I need."

"George, make her a pot," she said. "After all, this is your doing."

"No, really," I said. "I'm just going to reheat this morning's pot, if it's still there. It'll be fine." *I'll be miserable, but the coffee will be fine.* With my eyes trained on the floor, I practically ran to the kitchen.

"Try it this way," Rita said, moving my fingers down to the base of the artichoke. I'd been trying to get the hang of it for twenty minutes, but my hands weren't cooperating. As the sunlight glinted off my paring knife, I heard Burl Ives crooning "Silver Bells" from the parlor, and I knew George and his "friend" Iris were having a holly jolly time tossing back cider and throwing tinsel. Rita reached over and, like magic, extracted the booty from my artichoke. I didn't even realize I'd stopped working.

"Did you have to study cooking forever to get this good?" I asked.

"No," she said, mixing some kind of marinade. "School was just the beginning. The rest of it, the real learning, was on the job. Some of the best days of my life were spent toiling in hot kitchens for overly demanding chefs." She ground fresh pepper into the marinade. "Mostly in Montreal, but I did have a stint on Nantucket Island right before coming here."

I stopped pretending I was making any progress with the

artichokes and pushed them away. "You gave up Nantucket for
Islemorow? That's like giving up Hawaii for Coney Island."

"Not for me. It was just what I wanted—my own kitchen, my
own menu, my bedroom just across the hall. But you are the one
who is supposed to tell a story. Come now, about last night."

"Last night?" Damn, how could I talk about George without
revealing my wounds? As a stalling tactic, I picked up my knife
and attacked another innocent artichoke. After cutting off the
stem, I plucked the layers of green and yellow leaves, scooped
out the fuzzy stuff inside, and cut off the tough skin. Rita told
me I was doing fine, and then—*voilà*—the heart appeared. The
elusive heart. "Hey, I did it."

Rita took the nugget I'd worked so hard to find and handed me
another artichoke. "You have learned something important here."

"How to disembowel a vegetable?"

"Remember when we made the *pain d'amandes* dough. It
made you think you liked to cook, yes?"

I nodded.

"Then when it came to the harder things," she held up an
artichoke, "you thought it was pain in the ass, yes?"

I blushed.

"Here is the thing then," she said. "You cannot tell if
cooking is really for you when you only make what is sweet
and easy. You have to take on all of it, even the damn stinking
artichokes. Then if you still want to cook, you know you must
love it. Do you see what I am saying?"

I ruffled the artichoke leaves that were scattered on the
butcher block. Rita was saying more than she was saying, that
much I saw.

"It is all right," she said. "I can see you do not wish to talk now. You think it over. Maybe we will chat later."

"No, Rita, I do want to talk, really." This wasn't the truth, of course. I had no desire to discuss George, but I most definitely didn't want to get kicked out my safe place. "Let's—"

"I must start the meat now," she said, and I knew I was being dismissed.

My hand caught on a fistful of artichoke leaves. To get to my room, I'd have to walk through the parlor, where the party was in full swing. Maybe I'd hang out in the study until the shindig finished up. But who knew how long that would be?

"Are you all right, Penny?" Rita asked.

I turned my head bleakly toward the door. "I'm just not feeling like a party right now."

Rita eyed the door, me, and the door again. "Come." She walked over to the corner nearest the fridge and pushed the potted plant away from the wall, revealing a small door, maybe three feet high.

"This is the crawlspace I told you about," she explained, unlocking the latch. "The staircase inside leads to the broom closet on the second floor, a few doors down from your room."

Theoretically, this was a godsend. Realistically, it was the place where Mom had sensed something strange and where George had gotten hurt, hardly an attractive alternative to walking through the George and Iris lovefest. "Rita, I don't know."

She looked perplexed for a second, but it didn't take her long to catch on. "You do not think there is a goblin inside, do you?"

"No, of course not." There was no backing out of this now. "Just let me get my stuff." I retrieved my jacket and purse from the stool and returned to her side. "It's dark in there," I stated the obvious.

"I will keep the door open so you get some light. It will be fine."

It didn't feel fine. It felt like driving against traffic or ignoring a Beware of Killer Dog sign. But Rita was urging me on, and I really did hate the idea of walking through the party room. I took my first reluctant step inside, feeling suddenly far away from the shelter of Rita's kitchen. This was another world, a world between worlds, and I didn't belong in it.

"What about supper?" Rita asked. "The party could go on for hours."

The steps were squeaky, and I pretended not to hear her. I was too preoccupied with the concept of sneaking through an indoor cave to a bedroom that wasn't mine, to avoid a guy who wasn't mine, all because—well, I couldn't remember exactly why, and that made my head hurt, plus I felt spider webs on the back of my neck.

I forced myself to start climbing, slowly, warily, clinging tightly to the handrail. After a few uneventful steps, I kinda sorta relaxed, loosening my grip on the rail, quickening my pace. A hard shove on the door at the top and I tumbled into a closet filled with cleaning supplies and the smell of Pine-Sol.

🦋

Something unknown is doing we don't know what.
—Sir Arthur Eddington on the Uncertainty Principle in quantum physics, 1927

I barely got out of the broom closet and into the hallway when the Foxglove Room's door opened and Blue emerged, a smile brightening his bronze face, something round and wooden propped under one arm. "Blue, hi."

"I was just going to stop by."

"Perfect timing," I said, digging out my room key. "I've been wanting to talk to you."

We walked to my room and went inside. As we settled onto one of the loveseats, he set down what I now saw was a drum. "Is everything okay?" he asked.

"I don't know. I want you to tell me who your friend is."

He opened his mouth, closed it, crossed his ankles, uncrossed them, and finally said, "So you've met."

"Why didn't you tell me about her?"

"Starla doesn't like people. I thought she'd steer clear."

"Well, she didn't. You should've told me you had a girlfriend."

"Girlfriend?" he almost laughed. "She is most definitely not my girlfriend."

"Did she die in the fire?"

"No, she came here in the 1990s. Just showed up and never left."

"Not in any rush to cross over either then?"

"Something about wanting to wait for someone. She never really explained. And then it was too late."

Too late. So the cosmos enforced a deadline on crossing over?

Blue must have seen the confusion on my face, because he went on, "It has to do with her remains."

"You mean, her corpse?"

"Corpse, bones, ashes, a fingernail would probably do. Anything that remains of the body."

I nodded.

"The thing is," he said, "you can't cross over unless you're with some part of your remains. Your body is like a…a springboard, I guess you'd say. And while Starla was waiting for whoever she was waiting for, her ashes got scattered."

"Where?"

"That's the point. She doesn't know. The ocean maybe. Nowhere nearby, that's certain, or she'd feel it. That's one thing we ghosts have going for us. If our remains are in range, we know it."

"So she's stranded." God, how awful to be in limbo like that. To have died so young in the first place. "Is that forever?"

He shrugged. "She claims she'll never lose hope."

"No wonder she's clinging to you."

He let out a tense sigh.

"She loves you, you know."

Blue rearranged himself uneasily on the loveseat. "Actually, I think…well, I guess she could…what I mean is…look, can we talk about something else?"

"Okay, all right…let's, um, let's talk about your drum."

His whole face relaxed at that, and he lifted the hand drum onto his lap. "I found this on the beach a long time ago, forgotten or maybe abandoned. It's the only thing I've ever taken. It's the only thing I keep." He ran his fingers along the leather top and the wooden hoop, which was accented with small feathers. "I use it for journeying. The beat, you know. I thought we might, I thought I could show you. You said you'd like to know more."

"Uh, oh."

"Don't you trust me?" he asked, his voice partly Teasing Guy, partly Hurt Little Boy.

"I, um, hmm." Oh, what the hell. Maybe this journeying thing would help me understand what was going on around here. "Yes, I trust you. What do I need to do?"

"Close your eyes."

I did.

"Now calm yourself. Breathe. Try not to be thinking a thousand thoughts. Try not to think any thoughts."

"Impossible." At this point, I realized he was lightly tapping his drum, barely audibly, as if he were using a feather to strike it.

"That's okay, just try." He beat the drum a little louder, but still softly, a slow, steady pulse.

I listened to the rhythm. I took in a sudden salt air fragrance. I gave the not-thinking thing a try, but the thoughts came anyway, thoughts about ghosts, George, my mother.

And then I was gone. One minute I was sitting cross-legged on the loveseat, listening to Blue's hand against the drum, and the next minute I was somewhere else entirely. Somewhere dark and misty, tunnel-like and cold. I had the sensation of moving, but my feet weren't touching the ground. The thrumming of the drum was distant now. Was I dreaming? Hallucinating? Hypnotized? I wanted to call to the end of the tunnel in hopes that Blue was waiting there for me, but nothing came out of my mouth.

Suddenly, everything changed. The mist cleared, the darkness faded, the motion halted. I was under a bright—no, a searing—sun and a piercing blue sky, standing in a grassy, jungly place overlooking a crystal sea. There were a couple dozen kids—spring break types—walking around, poking their heads into what looked like cave openings. On a hill in the distance I saw an ancient stone structure, something that might once have been a temple or maybe a king's palace.

This can't be happening, I told myself. *You must have fallen asleep there on the loveseat.* But no, dreams were never this vivid. I could see every blade of grass, every twig and pebble underfoot. I could hear the individual notes of birds calling in the trees, smell the sunscreen on the tourists, feel the whoosh of the sea breeze.

Three of the spring breakers—two girls and a guy—wandered away from the others. They turned a corner around some rocks, out of sight of their group. They didn't seem to notice me, even though I was walking right next to them.

"Look," said one of the girls, pointing to a bunch of vines. "Let's go in." Her voice sounded kind of familiar, but I couldn't see her face behind her sunhat and shades.

"Go in where?" asked the other girl.

The first girl walked ahead and pulled back the vines to reveal the mouth of a dark cave. "C'mon," she said, flaunting a grin just before disappearing inside. I knew that smile.

"Hey you, wild woman," the guy said as he stepped into the cave. "Where are you taking us?" He put his hands on her shoulders. He was crushing on her.

"We're not supposed to do this, you know," the other girl said. "No going in the caves. No separating from the others." But she entered anyway, and—with the drumbeats echoing off the back of my awareness—I followed into the blackness.

The leader girl rifled through her shoulder bag and

The Black Butterfly

produced a flashlight. "Damn if I'm going all the way to Mexico and not exploring the Mayan caves," she said, taking off her hat and sunglasses.

Oh my God. No wonder her voice sounded familiar. She was my mother! My mother on her high school Spanish trip to Mexico. The trip that got her kicked out of private school. The trip that started her odyssey into Weird. I wasn't just in a different place—I was in a time warp.

Mom—well, she wasn't my mom here, not yet, for now she was just Vivian—directed the flashlight beam into the cave's interior. It stretched on forever. Here in the entryway, the cave was barely tall enough for us to stand upright, but in a short distance, it opened up to a high arching ceiling dripping with greyish brown stalactites. Rocky alcoves faded into shadow. I could see openings to side tunnels.

"Awesome," marveled Lover Boy.

Mom/Vivian flashed the light beam all around. "Remember what the tour guide said—how the Mayans thought caves were living things? I think they were right. Can't you feel it? It's breathing. Growing. Sweating even."

Lover Boy didn't miss a beat. "What I remember the tour guide saying is that caves are where the ancients went to screw and get high." He put his hand on Vivian's butt, but she slapped it away.

"I don't like this," said Scaredy Cat. "I'm leaving."

Vivian didn't seem to hear her, but Lover Boy did. "Come on, Babs," he coaxed. "Just a few minutes more."

"I'll see you later," she said, turning to leave. "And don't be late. I don't want to have to cover for you guys."

When she was gone, Lover Boy walked up behind Vivian

and put his arms around her waist. He tried to turn off the flashlight. He thought this was a hookup.

"Knock it off, Chance," she said, pulling the flashlight out of his reach.

"But this is the perfect place. Dark, private, roomy."

"This is sacred ground. If you'd pull your head out of your dick for once, you might get that."

His mouth opened, but he didn't say anything. He didn't know whether to feel amused, chastised or mad. Maybe she'd never talked to him that way. Maybe no one had ever talked to him that way.

"Chance," she said, her voice softening. "I really, really want to see what's here, and if we take more than a few minutes, we'll be missed. So let's just look around, okay? I'll make it up to you later, I promise." She stroked his cheek.

"Lead on then," he said in resignation, and she did.

We walked slowly, purposefully, awestruck by this vast, otherworldly place. It smelled dusty but not dirty, damp but not musty, old but not decrepit. In some spots, red and black line drawings adorned the walls, drawings of people or maybe animals, I couldn't tell. There was a secluded chamber to my left, and I had the creeping sense that if I looked inside, I'd find a thousand bats hanging from the ceiling.

All at once, Vivian stopped. Something had commandeered her attention. She stared into one of the stone alcoves, hand to her chest.

"Viv?" said Lover Boy. "What's going on?"

"There," she pointed, but he didn't see anything, and neither did I.

Somewhere outside, in the distant world of the above, a whistle blew. "That's us," said Lover Boy. "Time to hit the bus."

Vivian shook her head, her eyes still riveted to the empty alcove. The whistle blew again.

"Come on, Vivvy," he said, a nervous edge to his voice. "We've got to go."

"You go."

"Not without you." He tried to take her hand, but she shrugged him off.

"Go. I mean it." And she did mean it. Her voice was hard, urgent. She pointed the flashlight to the outside. "Tell them you don't know where I am. Tell them anything you want. Just go."

"But—"

"Please, Chance. I need more time. Do this for me."

He shook his head, but he did as she asked, leaving her all alone in the cavernous Mayan underworld. When she turned the light back to the alcove, I could finally see what she saw. There was a man squatting on the floor. A wizened, skinny old man wearing a toga-like shift, fanning a small fire. I don't know how I'd missed him before, how I didn't at least notice the flames and the shadows dancing on the rocky walls. He was so close to where we were standing, I could even smell the musky scent of him.

"Hello?" Vivian whispered.

He didn't look up.

"Habla español?" she tried again.

He turned his face toward the wall and said something, but it was neither Spanish nor English, and it wasn't directed at Vivian. He didn't know she was here. He reached into a small leather bag tied to his side and extracted a handful of powder, which he blew onto the fire. The flames jumped, and a spicy fragrance filled the alcove. He said something again.

The powder, whatever it was, made me feel strange, and it seemed to have the same effect on Vivian. Her eyes grew red and watery. She was unsteady on her feet and had to sit down. I joined her. It wasn't a disturbing sensation. In fact, I felt remarkably calm. Best of all, when the man spoke again, Vivian and I understood him.

"Granddaughter," he said, "do not be afraid. Do not be sad. This is a time to rejoice."

From behind us stepped a girl of twelve or thirteen, barefoot, dressed in a long white skirt and no top, just a white scarf tied in a way to cover her small breasts. She was beautiful, with dark green eyes, a black braid down her back, and beaded jewelry around her neck and ankles. When she stopped in front of the fire, she was fighting tears.

"Tomorrow is the day," the old man smiled up at her. "It will be a great and glorious time."

"I know, Grandfather," she said dutifully. "I know I should be happy and proud to join the gods who dwell here." She choked back a sob. "But I don't want to die! I don't want you to seal me in here until I perish from thirst and hunger and darkness. I don't want to sit alone among the bones of past sacrifices. I want to live!"

The poor girl. A human sacrifice. And what an awful way to go. Couldn't they just hurl her off a cliff and let her die instantly, instead of the drawn out agony of starvation? I looked at Vivian and saw sorrow in her eyes.

"You want to live," the old man said, blowing a little more powder into the fire. "And so you *shall* live. With the gods of the sun and the moon. Forever in glory." He offered her a toothless grin.

The girl was trying to look angry or at least indignant, but the powder was doing its job. She was sedate. The old man motioned her to sit, and he took her supple hand in his leathery one. "My child," he said, "your offering will assure us a bountiful harvest. You would not deny us that, would you?"

She lowered her head and shook it.

Vivian, red with outrage, was about to shout something, but she didn't get the chance.

"Vivian!" boomed a voice full of teacherly authority from outside. "Vivian Coltrane. Get your ass out here. You're busted."

That voice was all it took. The old man dissolved away, taking his granddaughter and his fire with him. Now it was just an empty, damp cave, filled with the echo of a teacher's threat.

Vivian stood up with difficulty. She looked out of it, hung over. "C-coming," she called hoarsely and stumbled out of the cave.

I tried to follow her, but I never reached the opening. Instead, I was suddenly back in the murky tunnel, alone except for the ever present drumbeats, which were louder now, coming from somewhere down the dim passageway. I felt cold and disoriented, but I walked on, knowing Vivian and the cave were inaccessible, walled off in another dimension. The door that had opened long enough for this one quick glimpse was shut.

I came to with a jolt.

"Welcome back," I heard Blue say, his voice as casual as if he were welcoming me back from a trip to the bathroom.

My head felt heavy and light at the same time. I had to look around to make certain I really was back. "What *was* that?" I asked when I was pretty sure I was in the right place and the right year.

"That was your first dream journey. How was it?"

"Are you kidding? Wild. How did you do it?"

"It's the drum," he said, toying with one of the decorative feathers. "The rhythm takes you beyond your five senses. A shaman would say the spirits escorted you. But you were still the driver. So it really wasn't me, it was you."

"Uh uh, no, I most definitely was not behind the wheel on that road trip."

"Maybe not consciously. Maybe it was deeper than that."

"But is it true, what I saw? Did it really happen?"

Blue shrugged. "I don't know what you saw."

"I saw my mother when she was—"

He held up a hand. "And even if you told me, I still wouldn't know if it's literally true, or just…true. Journeys are different for different people."

I slumped back into my seat. "I've always wanted to know what really happened to her down in Mexico. I still want to know."

He inched a little closer and said in an almost whisper, "I'll help you if I can."

Absently, I went to give his hand a squeeze. It didn't work, of course. "Sorry."

"Me too. I'd do anything if you could touch me like that. Like the way you meant it. Did you feel anything at all?"

"Well..."

"Nothing, huh?" He looked so sad.

"How about you?"

"Heat. Like a warm breeze maybe, but not like a human touch. I haven't felt a human touch in a hundred years."

"God, Blue. Well, at least we can see and hear each other. Am I really your first?"

He nodded, the backlighting in his eyes flickering. "Well, in a way, there was one other person, a young woman. I thought she saw me a couple of times in the hallway—you know, turning her head my way, slowing down when she got close. One night in the parlor, I could have sworn she was looking straight into my eyes. But then she walked right through me, like she had no idea I was there. No idea at all."

"How frustrating."

"I'll admit, I followed her around a bit after that, hoping she'd see me or hear me or *something*, but she didn't, and then she left. Her name was Vivian...Penny, are you all right? You look ill."

"Was this about fifteen or twenty years ago? And did she have wavy blonde hair and big teeth?"

"How did you know?"

"That was my mother, Blue."

His mouth unlatched and then curved into a vague smile.

"She may not have seen you, but she definitely sensed you," I went on. "She'd have done anything to make real contact with you. It's her dream, honest to God, her life's dream to see a ghost. She's in Idaho right now trying to track one down."

"Then I didn't just make the whole thing up. You both have the gift. Hers is just rougher."

It occurred to me that Mom wasn't much older than Blue when they almost met. They both would have been 20-something, even though one of them had been that way for decades. Twenty-something, good-looking, and desperately trying to connect with each other. "So, did you think she was cute?" I asked and then instantly felt appalled for saying it.

I don't know if ghosts ever blush, but Blue remained monochromatic. "I didn't look at her that way."

I made up my mind to believe him, not because I thought he was necessarily telling the truth, but because I couldn't stand the idea of him crushing on my mother, even if it was all those years ago. Why it bothered me, and why I was so eager to know if he'd had any love interests, was an egg I didn't want to crack. So I decided not to ask him anything else, for now.

"Hey, can we, um, pick this up a little later?" I asked. "I didn't get much sleep last night, and I'm beat all of a sudden."

"Of course." He stood up, drum in hand.

When he reached the door, he added, "I'll see you later." He said it like a question, like he didn't know whether I wanted to see him again or not.

But there was no question in my mind.

Chapter 5

Only two things are infinite,
the universe and human stupidity,
and I'm not sure about the former.
—*Albert Einstein*

When I woke up, my room was dark. What was supposed to be a catnap, just ten or fifteen minutes to recharge after my dream journey, turned out to be a two-hour doze on the loveseat.

My first impulse upon waking up was to call Mom, tell her about Blue, and ask her a zillion questions about Mexico. But no, if I did that, she'd be on the next flight out here, video camera in hand, giving credence to George's suspicions about me. God, that would be awful. I was not going to turn into Mom. No matter what.

My second impulse was to brood over George and his "friend" Iris. I was pretty sure I could entertain myself for hours with that one. I could beat myself up for letting myself believe he might turn out to be a nice guy. I could ask myself how I was going to face him over the next eleven days. I could list the personal defects that kept me from ever having a boyfriend. Yup, I could go on and on. However, right now I was hungry, since my lunch had consisted of a spoonful of bouillon topped with processed cheese stuff.

On the bright side, all seemed quiet below. Apparently, the

popcorn had all been strung, the virgin cocktails slung, and I wouldn't have to worry about crossing the tree-decorating party on the way to dinner. I hauled myself off the loveseat and headed downstairs. As I passed by the Tiger Lily room, I could hear Starla's voice. She sounded angry. No, not angry—urgent. I stepped closer to the door but couldn't make out any words, so I walked on.

The Christmas tree twinkled softly at the far end of the parlor. Tiny white bulbs and delicate, mostly glass ornaments wound their way tastefully around the branches, culminating in a silver angel at the top. I stood at the foot of the stairs admiring the unicorns and the gingerbread people, the little-boy handmade reindeer and the beaded balls, wondering what bits of family history each decoration held. I didn't even notice Bubbles lounging in a corner armchair, her legs dangling over one arm, a drink balanced on the other.

"There you are, Penny," she waved. "Feeling better?"

"A little," I said, stepping into the parlor. "The tree is gorgeous."

Bubbles nestled deeper into her chair and crossed her legs. "I think it's our best effort ever. That Olivia has a real eye for design."

"Olivia?" I asked.

"Iris's Olivia," Bubbles said. "Her partner. They've been together for ages, though not many people knew it the first couple of years. Didn't you meet her at the Grindle Point?"

I crumpled into the seat next to Bubbles as her words sunk in. All my misery, all my fake digestive illnesses, all my stupid behavior toward George this afternoon was even more ludicrous than I'd thought. "No, Olivia wasn't there," I finally said.

"Oh, too bad," she said, taking a sip from her glass. "Maybe another time."

"Maybe. Have you had supper yet?" I was suddenly too agitated to eat a thing, but it seemed like the polite thing to say, it being dinnertime and all.

Bubbles swung her legs around to the front and set her glass on the floor. "I ate way too many cookies to think about a meal. You go on ahead. I'm going to hit the hay early, I think."

I stood back up. "Okay, see you later." I started across the room, then thought of something. "Bubbles, would you mind if I used your computer for a few minutes? I have homework over the vacation, if you can believe it, and I need to look something up."

"Of course, dear," she said, motioning in the direction of the lobby. "It's right on the desk."

I googled *dream journey*. The first hit was Dream Journey Studio, a film company currently promoting its feature *Reiki: The Movie*. After that came a bunch of books, video games and songs with titles like "Dream Journey—The Last Unicorn," "Journey to a Dream" and "Dream Journey to the Peach Blossom Land." Not to mention the Huffy® Dream Journey "too cute" girl's bike with the "stylish pink frame and white tires."

When I typed *dreamjourney* as one word, that's when I got results. I learned that journeying is meant to "part the veils between the seen and unseen worlds." It's used for spiritual purposes like self-discovery, healing, sharing energy, and sensing a connectedness with others. Listening to drumming is supposed to slow your brain waves and help you enter the necessary altered state of consciousness.

Whoa, this stuff was freaky. I probably wouldn't have believed it if I hadn't just experienced it myself. But there was no denying that something remarkable had happened to me when Blue drummed, something unearthly and amazing. I read everything I could find online, then decided to see if there was anything else to read in the study.

I was already in the doorway of the study when I caught sight of George. He was taking the Monet print off the wall to reveal a flat-screen TV, and it wasn't until he sprawled on the couch with the remote that he noticed me.

"Hi," I said, hating that it came out squeaky.

"Hi," he answered. I just stood there, not knowing where to look or go, so he added, "You can come in if you want." Nothing in his voice said he *wanted* me to come in. All it said was *it's a free country*.

I walked over to the shelves and pretended to survey the books. Finally I gave up the ruse and sat on the far end of the sofa to watch him flip stations. *Mr. Magoo's Christmas Carol*, *A Very Brady Christmas*, *Chainsaw Noel*, the 24-hour Yule log, a holiday beauty product infomercial. Then finally success: *It's a Wonderful Life*, the movie about the underappreciated, overworked George Bailey, who's about to commit suicide until an angel shows him how bad his loved ones' lives would be if he'd never been born. I smiled as George Bailey promised Mary the moon.

"You like this junk?" George asked.

"I happen to love it. What's so terrible about liking a clean story with a happy ending?"

"Nothing." He sat up. "It's just that George Bailey spends his whole life putting himself out for other people and then

The Black Butterfly 115

resents it and doesn't take care of himself. I have no patience for people like that."

"Well, there's the holiday spirit."

"That's not what I mean," he said. "It's great what he does for others. But if it drives him to suicide, then what good is he to the people who count on him?"

This threw me a little off guard. As much as I wanted to disagree with George, I couldn't deny that he had a point here. Nor could I ignore how vividly green-blue his eyes shone when he spoke passionately about something. "Look, I'm a bit defensive about George Bailey," I said. "I guess I always dreamed of having a dad like him."

"Yeah, me too. I guess."

Deep down, way deep down, I believed my father actually *was* that kind of man, a George Bailey kind of man who'd have been a fabulous dad if only things hadn't gone wrong between him and Mom. But I would never say that to anyone, not ever.

We didn't speak much for the rest of the movie. George immersed himself in the story, and I tried to figure out how to convince him that I'm not a complete jerk. He sat politely through the Clarence the Angel scenes, and when everyone lived happily ever after and the credits rolled to the tune of "Buffalo Gal," he suggested making hot cocoa. I said okay, even though the knot in my stomach still had a death grip on my innards.

🦋

If you are not feeling well, if you have not slept, chocolate will revive you.
But you have no chocolate! I think of that again and again! My dear, how
will you ever manage?
— Marquise de Sevigne, February 11, 1677

In the kitchen, George swore I'd never had hot chocolate
if I hadn't tasted Belgian hot chocolate. He pulled out a
saucepan—a thick one, I learned, so the chocolate wouldn't
burn—and started poking around the pantry. "Ah, Callebaut
bittersweet," he said. "Perfect." Soon he was warming milk
and a vanilla bean in the saucepan, chopping up a mound of
chocolate, and setting out colorful ceramic mugs on the island.
I didn't know what to do with myself, so I grabbed a dishtowel
and started wiping up his crumbs. This made George laugh, and
I wondered if I'd swept chocolate dust onto my chest.

"Will you relax?" he said, taking the dishtowel out of my
hand. "This is a kitchen, not a still life." Then he told me to
watch the pot and let him know when bubbles started forming
around the edge. "We don't want the milk to boil."

I watched vigilantly. When a small orb of air appeared at the
edge of the pan, and then another, I called out, "It's bubbling!"

"All right, now for the fun part." Slowly, he added bits
of chocolate to the milk. As he whisked, the liquid changed
from satiny white to beige and then from russet to dark
chocolaty brown.

George tended the pan affectionately, like a painter
performing fine brushwork. I watched his hand, his arm and

his shoulder move with the precision of a dancer, losing myself in a daydream. We were slow dancing right there in the kitchen, without any music save the humming of the stove. Hand to hand, cheek to cheek, hip to hip. The daydream lasted until he took the pan off the flame, whisked it one last time to make foam, and filled our mugs to the rim.

Propped against the island, George took a mouthful of cocoa, closed his eyes, and tilted his head back. He seemed poised for a kiss. My lips were burning, even though I hadn't touched my steaming mug yet. George opened his eyes—now they were both sapphire—and asked in a velvety-chocolate voice, "Aren't you gonna try it?" So I did.

Wow. Wow squared. I once heard Dr. Ruth compare good chocolate to sex. Now I'd at least tried one of them. I took another sip and closed my eyes. It was so sumptuous, so creamy and pungent, like droplets of pure indulgence.

As I was about to lift the mug to my mouth again, eyes still closed, I sensed George moving closer to me. Wait, *was* he moving closer? Did I want him to? I didn't dare open my eyes. He was completely silent, but still I felt him standing nearer than before. Or was he?

"You like it?" he said so suddenly, so straight into my ear that I dropped my mug, which cracked on the floor and heaved its contents all over the place. I must have looked as mortified as I felt, because George instantly offered, "It's okay, it's only a cup. Watch your step. You didn't get burned, did you?" He picked up the broken pieces and then started wiping up the cocoa.

"I'm so sorry."

"No problem." He used his foot to swish the dishtowel over the chocolate puddle. "Almost done already."

"No, that's not what I'm sorry about." I dropped onto a stool. "I mean, I *am* sorry about that, but I'm even sorrier about this afternoon. About being so...not myself."

George stopped swishing and peered at me for a second before returning his focus to the floor.

"And I'm sorry I didn't stay at the lunch table," I continued.

He kept wiping. I wanted him to say something, anything, but he just continued making concentric circles with his foot, the towel, and the last licks of cocoa.

"Did I miss anything good?" I asked.

"Not much." He picked up the soaking dishtowel and tossed it into the sink. "Iris is transferring to her girlfriend's college next term."

I tried to look surprised.

"Buddy stopped by to say hi," he went on. "So did Mrs. Walker the Talker. Iris was worried about you, about your being gone from the table so long, but when I spotted you at the magazine rack, I figured you wanted some space."

My throat prickled with embarrassment.

"I have to tell you," he said, "I got the feeling you were really mad at me. Like, you were thinking the worst of me. Which seemed pretty mean."

I didn't know what to say, so I decided to borrow something someone else once said. "Never attribute to malice what can adequately be explained by stupidity."

"What?" He took off his sneaker and started rinsing the

chocolate-stained sole under the faucet. His sock had a hole at the big toe.

I joined him at the sink. "I made a mistake, a dumb one. But hey, James Joyce said mistakes are the portals of discovery."

"Can you please speak English?" he said, pulling his sneaker back on.

"Sorry, it's just, sometimes other people can say things better than I can."

"Don't you get it, Penny?" He straightened up. "I want to hear what *you* have to say." A drop of cocoa had formed on his upper lip, and he wiped it off with his thumb. "What *do* you have to say?" He took a single step toward me.

Suddenly I was all jittery. I was drawn to George and afraid of him at the same time, and it paralyzed me. He stepped back and said in a resigned voice, "Well, if you don't have anything to say, I do. I told you Iris was just a friend from growing up, but you didn't believe I was telling the truth."

"I—it's just that different people have different definitions of the truth, that's all," I said. Different definitions of *friend*, of *just happened to be there*, of *sweetie*. How was I to know Iris wasn't interested in him or any other guy?

"So I'm right—you thought I was lying."

"No, not lying. Just not necessarily telling me the whole story. Like I said, different people have different definitions of the truth." Unaware of what I was doing, I moved back a pace.

"Penny, what are you afraid of?"

"I'm not afraid. I don't know what I am, but..." I cleared my throat, hoping the right words would somehow find their way out, when to both my surprise and relief, the kitchen door swung open and there was Rita in her bathrobe and slippers.

"Oh, excuse me," she said. "I did not mean to interrupt. I just thought I heard a thud or something. Is everyone okay?"

"We dropped a mug," George said. "No worries."

"All right then. Good night." She turned to leave, but not without first tossing us a wink and a half-smile that might as well have shouted, "Looks like you two are getting cozy, after all."

"You've gotta love that woman," he said when she was gone.

I nodded my agreement, then yawned.

"You sleepy?" he asked.

"Not at all. I'm still just waking up from a major snooze."

"Hmm." He ran the faucet for no apparent reason, then turned it off. "Well, if you feel like it, we could go take a look at the tree. I haven't had a chance to, you know, take it in, give myself a pat on the back."

So he wasn't giving up on me. He wasn't going to force me to do any more explaining either. He was willing to move on. Which was probably more than I deserved.

"Sounds good," I said. "Yeah, show me what I missed."

"What's that?" I asked, pointing to a glass and rusty metal decoration. We were making our way around the tree in what George called a 360° inspection.

"Ma made that. It's supposed to be a boy skiing, but I always thought it looked more like a spider. See that one up there? That's the same boy ice skating."

"Where?"

"Almost at the top." He put one hand on my back and pointed with the other one.

"Oh, yeah…ooh, this one here is my favorite," I said, touching a handmade paper angel. The body was a toilet paper tube, the wings were cutout tracings of a child's hands, and the face was a school photo of a small George, complete with baby teeth and cowlicks.

He rolled his eyes. "Kindergarten project."

"It's adorable."

"It's toilet paper. C'mon, let's sit down."

So we did, right there. We sat on the marble floor and just admired the glittering tree, which seemed even taller and broader from this perspective. They must have spent hours trimming it. They must have had so much fun. Now every time they walked past it, they'd remember what a great time they all had together. And every time I walked by it, I'd remember how badly I blew it.

Eventually, I allowed myself to look over at George. His eyes reflected the tree lights in a kaleidoscope of twinkling greens and blues. When he blinked, the patterns shifted into a new collage, beautiful but unreadable. The stubble on his face was coming in red, I noticed, which surprised me but also pulled me in. I wondered how it might feel to the touch—spiky or downy, cool or warm? The questions made my fingers tingle.

George gave me all of three seconds to soak him in before he turned to face me. I didn't look away soon enough. He leaned in and whispered, "Whatcha thinking about?"

Damn, caught in the act. "I-I was just, you know, just…"

"The truth, please."

"Can't I pick dare instead?"

"Why, do you have something to hide?"

"No, of course not. All I was thinking was…" Should I tell him the truth? The *real* truth—that I was thinking about his body? Yeah, right. I could tell him *a* truth, but not *the* truth, no way. Not that, not yet.

"Well?"

"I was thinking how much fun I'm having here. How no one is more surprised about that than me, that's all. What about you—truth or dare?"

His mouth twisted into a smirk. "Dare."

Crap. I didn't want to concoct a stunt for George to perform. I wanted to discover who he was. I wanted to find out his deepest darkest secrets. I wanted to know what he was feeling this very minute. "Okay, smarty pants," I said, "I dare you to tell me why you're here alone."

George gathered his elbows to his sides as if he were trying to cushion himself from something. He rolled his tongue around in his mouth, then shrugged. "I was dating someone at school, if that's what you mean," he said. "But a couple of months ago she decided she needed a break."

"Do you hope she comes back?" I asked, not sure I really wanted to hear the answer.

"I think hope was invented by some ancient Greek slaveowner to keep the oppressed masses in a state of inaction."

"Pretty cynical there, George."

"If you must know," he began tapping his foot against the marble floor, "she did try to come back, and I told myself okay, it's not perfect, but maybe we'll be happy someday, and aren't I happier with that hope than with being alone?"

"And?"

"And then I realized I wanted someone I could be happy with right now." He deflected his eyes but then glanced back at me, and I saw the hope.

If only guys knew how appealing they are when they let their guard down. He reminded me of Tuna Breath when Gigi first adopted him: timid, trusting, willing. Suddenly my shadow self wanted to mold my body into a single shape with his. I wanted us to be a living, breathing, wrestling work of art, just the two of us.

Like *that* was going to happen.

My eyes dropped to his crescent moon pendant, which hung at an angle on his sweater. "Did she give you this?"

He lowered his chin to admire the necklace. "This? This was my birth mother's. Your turn."

I didn't want to play the game anymore. I wanted to keep talking, learning about him, trying to figure him out. But I didn't want to press too far either. "Dare," I said at last.

He stood up. "Kiss me."

"I want to change back to truth."

"Too late."

I wanted to kiss him—I really, really did, just not as part of some game. I wanted to be romanced, not dared, not watched. But maybe this *was* romance, George-style.

What if I disappointed him though? Making out with Charlie Warner a few times after school didn't exactly qualify me as a makeout expert. My kissing exploits had almost all been in my daydreams—imaginary guys giving me perfect, imaginary kisses. The question now was: could I kiss George the way I'd always longed to be kissed?

I stood up to join him, unsure whether I could do this. I stepped closer. He exhaled with a slight quiver in his throat. There was no running away now. No more chances to falter or laugh off the tension. It was time to act.

I raised my hands and cupped the back of his head. His hair, lush under my fingers, made me think of wild animals, of powerful cats and long-maned horses. On tiptoes, I lightly kissed his temple and behind his ear. His skin was electric. I let my mouth slip across his cheek, slowly, slowly, taking in each nuance of muscle and bone, until I reached his parted lips. He took over from there.

It was a long, deep kiss, our lips dovetailing over and over. I couldn't get enough. Kissing George was like taking that first forkful of a sumptuous meal when you're ravenous: peak pleasure and a maddening hunger for more. Smooth and spicy—like the ginger sorbet they were sampling at Whole Foods last month. Hot and chilling—baked Alaska. Sultry and tender—the ripest tropical fruit. There was barely time to breathe between helpings.

Much too soon, George lightened his hold on me.

"I hope you choose dare next," I whispered. "So I can dare you to kiss me again."

"Dare," he said, and his mouth pressed against mine once more. He caressed me with his whole body, it seemed, speaking in small sighs instead of words. Suddenly I was in the Chagall poster we have taped to our bathroom door in Cambridge, the one where the lovers are floating over the world, which has stopped turning just for them. When our kiss ended, George stayed wrapped around me. He glided us onto the sofa, where we wound ourselves into a ball, just holding each other, the Christmas tree lights twinkling over us like stars in Chagall's sky.

Chapter 6

I hate the outdoors.
To me the outdoors is where the car is.
—*Will Durst*

"It's January thaw come early," was how George talked me into the snowshoeing idea the next day just because the temperature had nudged above zero. One minute he was saying the snow looked perfect, and the next minute I was out back of the inn, wearing his oversized ski pants, fleece vest, down jacket, neck gator, and up-to-my-elbows mittens. He knelt to snap on my snowshoes, his hair falling over his red headband, then stepped into his own snowshoes and kissed me—a quick, warm peck—before taking a few effortless strides across the yard. "Ready?" he asked.

I lifted my left foot and moved it cautiously forward. When I tried to lift my right snowshoe, I realized—too late—that I'd stepped on it with my left one. Down I went on all fours. George helped me up and told me to try again. "That's right," he said when I'd managed to stay upright for a few steps. "Just keep walking. How do you feel?"

"Graceless and dorky." I stumbled for a few more paces until he wrapped a steadying arm around my shoulder.

"Well, you look great."

I kept my eyes on my feet and concentrated on not falling. Somehow in his agility George managed to keep our snowshoes from colliding with each other. When it looked like I was going to remain vertical, he let his hand slide down to the small of my back. He wasn't holding me up anymore—he was just holding me.

Eventually, I took my eyes off my feet and looked around. It was gorgeous out here, an ocean of snow followed by an ocean of water, covered by an ocean of pearly clouds. Being here with George, just the two of us, felt like sharing a secret—intimate, private, familiar. I looked at him, and he tightened his hold on me. In this winter light, his eyes were the richest blue, the boldest green, like the primordial blue and green from which all blues and greens evolved. Almost too strong to look at directly. Almost.

We zigzagged our way in the direction of the beach. "Too bad it's overcast," George said. "On a clear day, you can see Spruce Island."

"It's a great view anyway." The ocean was smooth and waveless, broken only by a pier and an occasional bird diving for a meal. Everything was so still, I thought time itself must be frozen over. It felt like we were far away from the inn and the rest of civilization, suspended here between ocean and sky, our own secluded alternate universe.

As we came to a stop a few yards from the water, I wondered if George's old girlfriend had ever stood here. Did she used to visit the Black Butterfly? Did they make love in his room or in the van or even right here on the beach late at night? A spasm of jealousy shot through my belly and rose to my chest, where it made me cough out loud.

Stop it, I told myself. *George is here with you—not the girl from college, not Iris, not anyone else. As hard as it is to believe, he has chosen you to bring to this very private place.*

This very private, very cold place. I loved being here, but I was cold now that we were standing still. I squeezed my arms and shoulders in an effort to stifle a shiver, but I shivered anyway.

"You're getting chilly," he said. "C'mon, let's head back home."

I opened my mouth to say okay, but before I could get the word out, a strange noise distracted me. Part yelp, part howl. I glanced in the direction of the sound and saw Starla standing on the pier. Her back was turned to me, but it was obvious that she was crying. She was wearing the same outfit as yesterday— no jacket, no gloves, no hat—and she was standing there bawling her eyes out.

George took a step back in the direction of the inn. "Let's go."

"Not yet," I said, my eyes locked on Starla. What was I not remembering about her? Something she'd said, but what? It seemed like something I should know. Something I'd want to know.

"Well, if we're going to stay out, we're going back to get you some more clothes," George said. "Come on—it'll just take a minute."

"Good idea, but I'll wait for you here, if that's okay. It'll be a lot quicker without me dragging down the pace."

He pinched his lips and looked like he was about to protest, but instead of saying anything, he kissed me and took off across the beach. When he was out of sight, I walked toward the pier.

"Starla?" I called.

She turned around, looking surprised and embarrassed.

"Starla, what's wrong?"

"It's B-Blue," she choked. "I think he…I just can't believe it…he…he…" She plunged into a sobbing bender and couldn't speak.

"Starla, please, tell me what happened."

"You've got to help him!"

I ran—well, my version of running, on snowshoes—onto the dock and headed toward her. If Blue needed help, I'd do anything. What I or any other mortal could do to help a ghost, I didn't know. But I'd do it once I found out from Starla.

I was almost at Starla's side. Just a few steps more. Maybe ten feet away from getting her to tell me what was going on. So close. So very close. Practically there.

In the first instant, I barely felt the boards beneath my feet start to splinter, hardly noticed the crackling of wood or the turning of my ankles. In the next instant though, I knew I was in trouble. A splinter became a fracture. The fracture became a gap. The gap became the doorway to a watery abyss. And then the planks gave way. Just before I disappeared into the icy sea, I craned my neck to see Starla. She was smiling wickedly at me, a stolen cordless saw in her hand.

At the moment I hit the water, I heard a thwack. It was a strange, hard clunk, not the kind of sound you're supposed to make in water. Could that be how a body sounds when it falls, snowshoes and all, six feet into the winter ocean? Or was Starla up to something? Stunned by cold and fear, I looked up to see if she was running the saw again, but she was gone, thank God. Now if I could just make it to shore.

My head started hurting before I could take a single stroke—really hurting, in quick, sharp jabs. I took off a mitten and touched the back of my head. My hand came back smeared with blood and strands of hair. "Oh, God," I whispered. I must have hit a rock or one of the fallen planks. That was the sound I'd heard. My heart began to pound, and as it did, it pumped fresh pain into my head.

"George?" I shouted. Nothing. I tried to swim again, but my legs and arms had turned to useless pieces of flesh. My nose tingled violently and then lost all feeling. "George?" I called one more time, then shut my eyes. "Please," I breathed to no one.

I was sure I was going to die right there, a stone's throw from the beach. But when I had my eyes closed for a few seconds, the strangest thing happened: I started to feel a little better. My hysteria downgraded to anxiousness, my pulse slowed a notch, and the stabbing in my skull eased a bit. Red and black starbursts floated in front of me, then blew away. Most amazing of all, the water wasn't so terribly bitter anymore, now that I was used to it. In fact, it was sort of invigorating, as long as I didn't get the salt water near my cut head.

How can this be? I wondered. *My jacket and mittens are already iced up, yet I don't feel cold anymore. I feel good.*

I swam a few strokes out into the ocean, then a couple more, and then I turned back. Alone in winter was not the right time for me to go swimming in strange waters. Besides, I needed to get this gash cleaned up. I pressed my fingers to the cut place, hoping the blood was drying, but it came off wet and fresh in my hand. "Damn. Where is he? George, where are you?" I said, but not too loudly. I could wait a while longer for that extra jacket. I really wasn't ready to get out of the water anyway. It was so tranquil here in the ocean, like a warm bath. No, like a comfortable bed. Or a home. That was it—it felt like coming home to a warm bath and a comfortable bed.

"Bed. That's what I need," I affirmed as a wave of fatigue overtook me. "Right after I get cleaned up. Bed and a good night's sleep."

I looked up at the pier. The platform was higher than I'd expected. Had I really fallen that far? Could I manage to climb back up? I was so tired all of a sudden. Too tired. Maybe I could take a rest right here…

I must have fallen asleep there in the water, because the next thing I knew, I was in someone's arms. "Penny?" he said. "Penny?" I didn't recognize the voice at first, but it was male and it was urgent. I, on the other hand, only wanted to be alone and drowsing. "Penny!" he said again, and I felt his hand on the back of my head, which was tender to the touch. "Penny, wake up."

My mouth felt rubbery and warped, too clumsy to make words, but I tried. "Dun wanna," I sputtered. I'd been having a delicious dream. I dreamt I was going to live in the ocean, that I was already making a coral bed for myself and learning how to breathe water. Waking up, the air seemed too thin for my lungs, the atmosphere too dry. I wanted to go back to my new home.

"Penny, stay with me," he demanded. Then gently, "Please."

My eyelids were cooperating about as well as my mouth, but I managed to get one of them open. "Who…?" I started but couldn't finish.

"Shhh," he said. "You don't have to talk. Just be awake. Be here."

With effort, I got my other eye to open. Now I just had to get both eyes to work together. Why was everything so blurred, so spinning?

He cradled the back of my head more snugly and lifted me to his bare chest. "Take a deep breath," he said.

My eyes closed again. I longed for my coral bed.

"Penny!" he ordered. "Look at me…good, now breathe."

I opened my mouth and sucked in the thin, dry air. "Blue?"

"You can see me now—good."

"I've always been able to see you, remember?"

He lowered his face until his nose was practically touching mine. "Not ten minutes ago, you couldn't."

"You've been here for ten…?" I couldn't get the rest of the words out. I felt so strange.

"Keep listening to my voice, Penny. Keep looking at my face."

I leaned my head against his chest and gazed up at him.

"I know what happened," he said. "I'm so sorry."

"I'm glad you came," I said. He looked taller than I remembered, his face almost touching the clouds. "Hey, would you do something for me, a favor?"

"Anything."

"Would you tell Starla…tell her…tell her…"

"Don't worry, I know exactly what to tell her. I'll take care of her. Right now, why don't we just enjoy the water together, just for a little while longer. Look, the moon is up."

I turned my head skyward to see a full yellow-orange ball hanging low in the sky. How had it gotten so dark out?

"Nice, huh?" he said. "It's a blue moon tonight."

I squinted. "Looks kind of red to me."

He touched my face. "Yes, but blue moon means it's the second full moon this month. An extra full moon. Happens once every few years." His fingers were tracing the hollow of my neck with a light, swirling motion.

"You know what I like best about the moon?" he went on. "I like how it melts right into the ocean. Look. Look straight out there. Doesn't the water's surface look like a moon spill?"

I looked at him, at his warm brown eyes, and then out where he was pointing. He was right. Silvery threads of moonlight, like a soft blanket, glimmered on the water's surface as far as you could see. A blanket of moonlight. I wanted to lie under that blanket and stare at the sky forever.

"It's not that way with the sun," he said. "The sun turns the ocean colors, blue or sometimes green, but it doesn't get into the water, not the way moonlight does." He pulled me a little closer. "It doesn't get inside."

For a while, we watched the sky without talking. At last, I said, "Look at that bright star next to the moon. It's so big."

"That's because it's not a star. It's Jupiter. Now, see over there, lower in the sky and not as bright?" He repositioned me so I could see. "That's Saturn."

I liked being in his arms, having him hold me, having the water hold me too.

"Penny, open your eyes," I heard him say. "Penny!" He jostled me a little, and I obeyed. "How about I tell you a story?" he asked. "Will that keep you awake?"

"Mmm, make it a long one," I said, tipping my head back into the water, happy to discover that the salt no longer stung my wound.

"I'll tell you a tale I learned from one of the men I fished with, an Inuit man," he said. "It's about Sedna, a girl who lives in the ocean."

A girl who lives in the ocean. I envied her.

"Sedna lived even farther North than here," Blue said. "One day, a giant seabird promised her a palace to live in if she would be his bride, so she climbed onto the bird's back and flew across the sea. But the so-called palace was only a nest on a cliff where the bird kept her imprisoned day and night. She was miserable. Thankfully, her father kayaked across the sea and rescued her."

"Nice to have a father who cares," I mused.

"I'm sorry?"

"Nothing. Go on."

"Well, as Sedna and her father rowed back home, the seabird suddenly appeared. The creature tossed Sedna into the water and then pecked off her fingers when she tried to climb back into the kayak. Her fingers grew into the first whales and seals. Then she sank to the bottom of the ocean, where she became the goddess of all the sea creatures forevermore."

"Forever at the bottom of the ocean," I repeated longingly.

Blue's face grew grim. "Don't say that."

"Why not? It's beautiful down there. So quiet, so dark."

"Stop it, Penny."

"Okay, fine. Let's change the subject. Hey, I noticed you've been practicing."

"Practicing what?"

"Holding living things." I pushed my spine into his upper arm. "You're doing great."

"No."

"What do you mean, no? You've been holding me this whole time. That's fabulous."

Blue's forehead screwed up into a knot, and the color drained from his face. His jaw was working overtime.

"Do you mean…?" I didn't really need to ask. I knew perfectly well what he meant. I glanced over at the pier. It was supposed to be just a few feet away, but it seemed like leagues. The shore was nowhere in sight. It was just Blue, the ocean, the planets and me. I pointed in the direction of the beach. "I'm not going back there, am I?"

"I don't know." His voice was cracking.

"The fact that you're able to hold me right now—doesn't that mean I'm already dead?"

"You feel that way, you look that way, but I don't think you are. Your spirit is still inside you. You have a chance."

"What percent chance?" I asked, making no effort to hide my boredom with this angle of the conversation. "Exactly… what…percent…"

"Penny!" he said, patting my cheek, and it was only then that I realized my eyes were closed once more.

"I know, I know. But I can't make it back there by myself. Will you take me?"

His chest heaved. "I cannot. If you go the route of life, I won't be able to carry you anymore. My hands, my arms, will go through you. I'll be useless. You'll sink."

This was interesting, but somehow not interesting enough to coax me to open my leaden eyelids. "So, okay," I slurred. "So I can either drown…or…"

The next thing I knew, I was lying on the pier, coughing up seawater and feeling like I had a pickaxe lodged in my skull. I was so incredibly cold, so strangely disoriented. My hair and all my clothes were coated in ice. I couldn't catch my breath. I was terrified, although I didn't know why.

"Penny! Penny, are you all right?" he asked. Only it wasn't Blue. "Penny," he shouted. "Penny, I'm here."

"George?"

When he saw that I could breathe and talk, he sighed, "Thank God," and pulled me to him. He was wet and cold too. "Jesus, Penny, I thought you were…how did this happen? I never should have left you alone, not even for the five minutes it took me."

"Five minutes?" I wheezed through chattering teeth. "That's not right. The Sedna story alone took five minutes."

"The what? Never mind. It doesn't matter. As long as you're okay. *Are* you okay?"

"Sort of. I want to go inside." I tried to stand up but could only get as far as my hands and knees.

George took my arm and helped me up. Fortunately, he didn't seem to notice my gash. The water must have washed the last of the blood away.

"My snowshoes," I said. "Where are my snowshoes? I'll need them to —"

"I took them off. You aren't walking. Come on, climb on my back."

"I'm all right. I can walk."

"No," he said so severely that I didn't try to resist. He bent over, and I climbed on—me and about ten pounds of water and ice. I don't know how George did it, but he carried me—a waterlogged sack of potatoes—on his soaked back all the way to the inn. With each step, I could feel his lungs, shoulders and legs laboring. At one point, he had to stop to catch his breath and wipe the ice off his face. I'd have felt sorry for him if I hadn't been so focused on not sliding off.

George brought me in through a side entrance and set me down while he took off his snowshoes. The shock of warm air felt so good, I wanted to cry. Even more than that, I wanted to get out of my icy clothes. So, with our arms around each other, we lugged ourselves up a back staircase and into my room, where we shook the icicles out of our hair and kicked off our boots. Then George ran the Jacuzzi for me. I sat in front of the hearth and tried to unzip my jacket, but my fingers were too numb.

"Need some help?" he asked on his way back from getting the water going. He'd already taken off his outerwear and shirt and was standing there in nothing but his black jeans. I swallowed hard.

"I think I'm okay," I said, an obvious fib. My hands were marmalade. But still, I didn't feel ready for George to undress me—not like this, anyway.

"Come on," he said, kneeling in front of me and starting to work on my socks. "This will be strictly clinical, I promise. Out of the ice suit and straight into the tub, okay?"

What could I say? I was a ragdoll.

George pulled off my jacket and ski pants, then my jeans, sweater and turtleneck, leaving me in my nowhere-near-cute-enough bra and panties. At least my legs were shaved.

When the last non-underwear item came off, I announced,

"I can get it from here." I wasn't sure this was true, but the feeling was coming back to my fingers a little. I went into the bathroom, where a steaming bath was waiting for me. Not just any bath—a bubble bath. "You know what?" I called. "I haven't taken a bubble bath since...I actually don't think I've ever taken one."

He came to the doorway. "I was hoping the bubbles would help you say yes if I asked to take a shower." He nodded to the standalone shower beside the tub.

"I, uh...sure." Well, why not? He was as cold and wet as I was, after all.

George looked slightly surprised—happy, but surprised. I wondered, was he surprised that I agreed, or that I agreed so readily?

"Just, give me one minute, would you?" I asked.

"You got it," he said, grabbing a towel before closing the door behind him.

I got out of my skivvies and into the hot water, which hurt like hell at first, then felt heavenly. My skin started to pink up immediately, and I decided I never wanted to go outside again. "Okay, George, c'mon in."

When he opened the door, he was wearing only a towel and a bashful smile. "Hi," he said.

"Hi."

"I'll, um, get to work here." He stepped into the shower and pulled the curtain around him before removing his towel and starting the water.

I sank a little deeper into the tub as the room filled with fresh steam. Try as I might to keep my mind empty, to simply soak up the heat and the moisture around me, I couldn't do it. I couldn't stop thinking about George, just a few feet away from me, separated by nothing more than a thin curtain. I'd seen enough of him by now that it wasn't too hard to fill in the blanks. He was beautiful, and now he was wet and naked too, his silhouette swaying and flexing hypnotically before me.

Suddenly the shower curtain opened and a towel-clad George reappeared. I wondered if I'd fallen asleep—I didn't even hear the water stop. "Already?" I asked.

"That's all I needed. Take your time though. Soak."

"No arguments there. But stay. I...want you to stay."

"Okay." He tightened his towel and knelt down beside the tub. His eyes were saying something too fragile for words, something hushed and important. It didn't matter that I couldn't translate the message. I just liked watching him send it. "Now will you tell me what happened?" he asked.

I took his hand and squeezed it. "Let's not think about that. It's done. You saved my life, and I owe you everything. Now let's move on."

"You don't owe me anything. I'm the one who left you alone out there, remember? You could've died because of me. I have to live with that knowledge, and it would really help if I could just understand what happened."

"I don't know, George. I walked out on the dock—for the view—and the boards collapsed right under me. I don't remember anything else. Just that it hurt." This was a bald-faced lie. I may have had trouble remembering my first encounter with Starla, but not this one. Something clicked this time, and all the details of her murderous plot sat indelibly in the front of my brain.

"Maybe we should get you looked at."

"Get the dock looked at. I'm fine."

"Are you really?"

"This bath was the perfect thing. I think I'm ready to get out now." Another lie. I could have soaked for hours, but I couldn't deal with any more questions.

"Okay, all right. I'll give you some privacy."

But I didn't let go of his hand. Instead, I pulled it to my cheek. Slid his fingers down to my neck. Past my shoulder. Over my collarbone. Onto my breast, still hidden behind the bubbles. I guess the whole near-death experience gave me some mettle.

"Can you feel my heartbeat?" I asked.

He didn't say anything, but I knew he felt it. My heart was palpitating.

"I can feel yours too," I said. "In your fingers."

He glided his hand to my ribs, my belly. I flinched when he hit the ticklish spot near my bellybutton. We kissed. Nuzzled. Breathed. Then, with one final brush of my cheek, he stood up. "You'll be okay getting out?" he asked.

"I think so. If I need you, I'll pull the emergency chain." I pointed to the chain-pull toilet, which made him laugh.

While I dried off, got into my robe, and lightly blew my hair, George went to his room to dress. He scared up an electric blanket too and was putting it on my bed when I emerged from the bathroom. I took one look at the four-poster and knew I'd been born to crawl into it. I was ready to drop—beyond exhausted and starting to feel disoriented again.

"All set," he said, plugging in the blanket. He pulled back the covers, and I fell in. "Get some rest," he ordered.

"Are you going to…" I started. No, that's not what I meant to ask. "Did he tell you what she tried to…" Oh no, what was I saying?

"Shhh," he said. "Just sleep. I'm leaving your door unlocked so I can check on you later."

"You won't tell Rita or Bubbles about this, will you?"

I was asleep before he could answer.

When I woke up, Blue was standing at the foot of my bed, his arms crossed and his eyebrows knotted.

"You can walk through walls?" I croaked.

"No, George left the door unlocked."

For a moment, I didn't even remember how I'd gotten into bed, or why. Then everything came crashing in on me. "Will you make me a…" I had no idea what I was saying. "I mean…wait, yeah, are you standing guard in case Starla tries to kill me again?"

"Starla will be leaving you alone from now on," he said. "I promise."

I pulled the electric blanket up to my chin. "What makes you so sure?"

He unfolded his arms and came over to my side. "She and I have come to an understanding."

"Starla doesn't seem like the kind of person you can…" I couldn't find my thought. "…the kind of person you can negative—I mean, negotiate. The kind of person you can negotiate with."

"Negotiating had nothing to do with it. It was more like a…"

"A thread?" I asked, vaguely aware that it was the wrong word.

"Something like that." Looking to the door, he said, "Someone's coming down the hall—probably George."

"What should we do?"

"Nothing. He won't see me. I'll leave when he opens the door. Just act like I'm not here."

"When will I see you?" I asked. He didn't answer, so I added, "Bring your...thing. That thing you tap, okay?" What was wrong with me?

When George came in, I pretended to be asleep for fear of what I might let slip this time. He set a glass of water on the nightstand, straightened my bedcovers, stroked my cheek. He'd saved my life, and now he was nursing me back to health.

Chapter 7

A photograph is a secret about a secret.
The more it tells you, the less you know.
—Diane Arbus

I woke up around 3 a.m. with a nasty lump on the back of my
head and muscles the consistency of jello. "Hello?" I rasped
into the blackness. No response. Still, I didn't dare assume that
I was alone—my door was unlocked, after all. "Starla?" What
I needed to do was force myself up to lock the door. Instead, I
rolled over and fell back to sleep.

When I woke again, it was just past eight. Beyond the
valances and the frosty windows, the sky glowed all pink and
gray. The sun hid behind the pine trees, shooting little jewels
onto the snow. The lustrous light made it look almost mild
out there, but I wasn't fooled. It was bitter cold outside—and
lusciously warm under the blankets. I had no desire to get out of
bed, no desire and very possibly no capacity. I was still so tired.

I reached over and took *Facts and Fancies* off the nightstand.
Yes, I thought as I propped myself up with pillows, *a little reading,
a little picture gazing, and then I'll either get up or go back to sleep.* It
was still early, after all, and besides, what else did I have to do?

According to Alda M. Eldenberry, the birds I saw yesterday
were diving ducks—either Oldsquaw or goldeneye, which

are the "only feathered friends hearty enough to endure our winters." In springtime though, "the island is flush with the songs of warblers, sparrows and thrushes, while summer brings guillemots, eiders and laughing gulls."

I learned that the island has no squirrels (just as I'd suspected), rabbits or raccoons, and that there are public toilets at the wharf, the Grindle Point Shop, and, seasonally, Katie's Salon Divine. There are no liquor sales, but efforts to make the island smoke-free have failed.

I found photos of lobstermen, beach bathers, maple sugarers and quilters. Sailboats, snow forts, pickle barrels and wedding cakes. Stolen kisses and champagne toasts. But the picture that really caught my attention was a black and white photo of a young man—maybe still a boy—hammering nails into the frame of a house that was going up. He was shirtless and smiling brightly, as if he were enjoying the workout. The caption said: "Tommy Klingler, of the A&J Klingler Building Contractors family, died a few weeks after this photo was taken, circa 1916, when he fell off the roof of the house being built for painter Cleo Easton. Construction on the site was halted for nearly a year, eventually being completed by a contractor from Massachusetts."

Another tragedy in this place. Poor Tommy Klingler. I stared at his smiling face for a long time, wondering what he had for breakfast that day, if he had a best friend, whether it scared him to perch so high on those wooden beams. I even imagined a life for him, the life he'd have had if not for the fall. He'd have fallen in love with a hot daughter of Cleo Easton, eloped to the Bahamas, stayed on to build spas and luxury homes in the islands, and made love to his wife every night on the beach. Poor Tommy. It would have been a great life. Why did he have to fall? Because life's a bitch and then you die, apparently. I closed the book and my eyes.

When I finally had the oomph to get up and get dressed—slowly, achingly—I headed downstairs, making certain to lock my door first. I listened for voices outside the Tiger Lily and Foxglove Rooms but heard none. Looking behind me every couple of seconds, I finally made it to the parlor, where I found George fiddling with the Christmas tree lights. He didn't notice me, so I stood behind him and took a couple of moments. One moment to catch my breath—I was still wobbly—and one to admire the rear view. Then I touched him lightly on the shoulder.

"Hmm?" he said, turning around and taking a red bulb out from between his lips. "Hey, you're up." He kissed me lightly. "How you doing?"

"Pretty...uh...well. Watcha up to?"

"Just fixing some distressed decorations. Then I've got to help Mike Smitty cut back some branches that've been dangling over the roof since last week's storm."

"So he found his cordless saw?"

"Guess so. Hey, you must be hungry after missing supper last night. How about I walk you to the dining room?"

Alone in an unlocked room? No thanks. Not before I'm strong enough to run for my life. "That's okay," I said. "Not sure how much longer I can stay vertical anyway. I just wanted to say hi. I'm gonna head back upstairs."

"Take my arm," he said, offering me his elbow. "You look like you could use an escort."

Escort? Bodyguard was more like it.

All secrets are deep. All secrets become dark. That's the nature of secrets.
—Cory Doctorow, Someone Comes to Town, Someone Leaves Town

As soon as George and I rounded the top of the curved staircase, I spotted Blue sitting next to his drum outside my room. I was relieved to see him—to know I wouldn't have to be alone—but I couldn't show it, not in front of George.

"You'll be okay?" George asked when we reached my door. "You look a little...washed out."

"I'm fine, just tired. Don't worry."

He leaned in to kiss me, but I couldn't do it with Blue sitting right there. Not a real kiss, a lover's kiss. In a preemptive strike, I reached up and planted one on his cheek. Just a peck, a thanks for walking me home kind of kiss. "Be careful out there," I said, turning to unlock the door. "Come by later?"

"Definitely."

"Good." I opened the door, and Blue followed me inside. "See you later."

Once inside, I fastened the lock and leaned my full weight against the door. The simple act of climbing the stairs had depleted me, and so had that uber-weird threesome. I was thankful to be back in my bolted fortress, where I was safe from Starla and free to acknowledge Blue. "Hi," I said wearily.

Blue walked over to the hearth and sat cross-legged on the floor. "How are you feeling?"

"I'm fine," I said, dropping onto the floor with him. "I

mean, I'm sore and tired and still weirded out, but I'm fine."

He raised an eyebrow of doubt.

"Okay, all right," I said. "Maybe I'm not fine yet, but I'll be fine, really." *If I can survive long enough.* "How about you? How has your day after been?"

"My day? Hard to say." He lifted his drum onto his lap. "Time doesn't pass like that for me anymore—yesterday, today, a beginning in the morning, an end at night. It's more like a long road that doesn't go anywhere. At least, that's how it was until you got here."

The muffled drone of a saw buzzed from somewhere overhead. "George and Mike Smitty are taking care of a branch," I said, hoping to change the subject.

He started drumming, slowly at first, then picking up the tempo after a minute.

"I like that," I said.

"I'm glad."

"The dream journey I had, it was so real. Like I was right there with my mother in Mexico, seeing, hearing, feeling everything she did."

"Was it unpleasant?"

"Not at all. It was amazing." I closed my eyes and focused on the cadence of his music. He slowed the rhythm again, until I found myself waiting longingly for the next beat.

"I haven't seen Starla today," he said. "Is she…"

I didn't hear the rest of his question.

This time there was no misty tunnel or dizziness, just the beat of the drum and the sensation of motion. I felt Blue next to me, and then I didn't. I was transported.

I found myself in a dark, windowless room, lit only by garlands of glow sticks and a disco ball. Forty or fifty people were hanging out, dancing to tunes on a boom box, hitting the chips and soda, trying to talk over the noise. When my eyes adjusted to the dimness, I saw that most of the people—girls *and* guys—had heavily made-up faces complete with lipstick, mascara and blush. One of the girls, decked out in neon green eyelids and orange lips, walked up to one of the guys and said, "Feed me, Seymour." He stroked her hair and asked, "Does it have to be human?" "Feeeeed me!" she replied.

Had Blue drummed me into a slasher bash or what? I was looking for the nearest exit when my eye caught the poster taped to the cement wall: "Bangor High School presents *Little Shop of Horrors*." Thank God. I wasn't at a perv meetup. I was at a cast party in some kid's basement. I took a deep breath and wandered over to the snack table, since it was at the opposite end of the room from the boom box.

Seymour and the orange-lipped girl were still role playing when another guy joined them. "Hey, Audrey," he said, "I think someone slipped your sister a mickey."

Audrey lost her Broadway smile and grabbed the guy's arm. "What? Where?"

He pointed to a grungy couch pushed against the wall, where a girl was curled up, her hair dangling over her face, a plastic cup lying on her lap, dripping Coke onto her jeans. The girl looked younger than me, and she was clearly pregnant.

"Jeezus F-ing Christ!" Audrey said. She ran over to the couch and shook her sister's shoulder, but the girl was out cold. "Wake up already, will you?" she muttered, lightly slapping her sister's face. Then suddenly Audrey was screaming. "She's not breathing! Call 911! My sister's not breathing!"

Someone killed the boom box, and the room turned silent. Audrey started blowing air into her sister's mouth and then pushing hard on her chest with both hands. "Come on, come *on*," she panted. Now I joined the crowd circling the sofa, wishing there was something I could do. Only then did I see who Audrey's sister was: Starla.

Something happened to the room then. Or maybe to me. The air turned cold and windy. Blue's drumbeats rang in my ears, faster and harder than before, like an emergency, like the racing of my pulse. Everything was vibrating. And then everything was still and warm again.

I was in a hospital, standing outside a neonatal unit. Big sister Audrey and another girl where there too, peering through the window at the baby in the incubator. The tiny thing was attached to all kinds of tubes and monitors, and his eyes were bandaged shut. From one corner of his high-tech bassinette hung a necklace with a pendant shaped like a crescent moon. *A crescent moon.*

Audrey rested her forehead against the window and stared at the preemie. "He's so tiny."

"He's beautiful," said her friend. "You have a beautiful nephew."

Audrey put a fisted hand on the window and nodded. "I just wish they'd saved Starla instead of him."

The friend massaged Audrey's shoulders. "They didn't have a choice, kiddo. It's a miracle they didn't both die. You know that, right?"

Audrey didn't answer. Or maybe she did—I don't know. Suddenly I was back in the Lilac Room, trying to breathe. All at once, I knew. I knew who Starla was waiting for. I knew why she came to the Black Butterfly. She wanted to be with her son. With George.

"Steady now," I heard Blue say. "You're back. You okay?"

"Uh…huh."

Why didn't Starla want Blue to know she was a mother? Was she afraid he'd see her differently? Should I tell him? I wanted to—I wanted to tell him everything I'd learned. And why shouldn't I? It wasn't like I owed Starla her privacy or anything else. And yet…

"Can I ask you something?" I said.

"Anything."

"Do you have feelings for Starla?"

"Yes—murderous ones. Are you kidding? She almost killed you."

"But before that. Before I came here. Did you like it? Did you like knowing someone loves you?"

He ran his fingers over the top of the drum. "It's one thing to be loved. It's another thing to be loved by the person you desire." His gaze slipped down to my lips.

I felt an ache, a sadness that frightened me. I'd seen it before, the way he was looking at me. Heard the misery in his voice. Felt the strong, hungry way he held me in the ocean yesterday. But I hadn't let myself dwell on these things because…because it was just easier that way. After all, if I accepted the fact that Blue had feelings for me, then I'd have to sort out how I felt about him.

He half-smiled at me. I knew I had to say something, but I couldn't form a distinct thought, much less put it into words. "Blue, I...I mean...it's like..."

"It's okay."

"No, it's not. It sucks."

"What sucks," he whispered so quietly I had to lean in to hear him, "is that I just heard the Tiger Lily Room door open. She's probably eavesdropping right now."

"Damn her," I whispered back.

"I'd better go."

"Why?"

"I don't know. I just think it's the right thing for your sake."

"So you're not convinced she's going to leave me alone."

His vast brown eyes pierced mine, but he said nothing.

"I hate letting her dictate," I said.

"You should get some rest. I'll deal with Starla." He stood up and gave me one last lingering look. As I watched him slip out the door, I wondered how Starla was going to make me pay for seeing him again. Then I got up and locked the door.

Chapter 8

Cooking is like love. It should be entered into with abandon or not at all.
—Harriet Van Horne

I curled up in a corner of the brown sectional couch in the lobby, watching George get the fire going. It was late, but I was wide awake. Once Blue left my room this afternoon, I'd fallen sound asleep and stayed that way until George made me come down and try to eat some supper. After that, we sat at the lobby desk and looked at his family photos and the CIA web page on the computer. Now we were the only ones still up, so we decided to move to the sofa. It was actually starting to feel like a normal evening, and the massive gnarl in my belly was thinking about unwinding. Maybe Blue had actually injected some sense into Starla. Maybe things would be all right.

"How'd the branch-cutting go, by the way?" I asked.

"A breeze—Smitty sent me down after five minutes. Guess my manual skills are better suited to a spatula than a power saw."

"I think your manual skills are exquisite."

He laughed, and I wondered: was he thinking of the same things I was? Of how tightly he held me the first time we kissed by the Christmas tree? Of my bubble bath, when he traced my body with the softest of touches? Of the way he stroked my cheek when he put me to bed under the electric blanket?

He nudged the poker between the logs until a single,

thin flame rose, like a skinny red cat stretching after a nap. Eventually, a few more puny flames woke up to join the party. George didn't have Vincent's or Blue's knack with the fireplace, but it didn't matter. There was no shortage of heat when we were in the same room.

"Come on, sit with me already," I said.

"I have to get something in the other room first. Be right there."

I lay my head back and watched the fire's reflection in the skylight, the flames seeming to lick the frost on the glass. In my mind, I saw the smiling face of Tommy Klingler, whose own light didn't get to shine for nearly long enough, his roof-fall death so unfair, so purposeless. He never got to grow up, do crazy things, do great things, do anything. I blinked hard. Tommy's smile faded from the skylight, leaving only the flames. Now I saw the Legacy on fire. Blue was falling into the raging flames, holding a dead baby.

No, Penny, I chastised myself. *Block it out. This is your night to be with George. Don't go there.* I closed my eyes and let the warmth of the room embrace me. *You can do this. For once, you can be right here in the moment.* When I opened my eyes, George was back, carrying a platter.

"Ready for a midnight snack?" he asked.

He'd made fondue! George had cooked for me, just like he promised. He'd used those magnificent hands with all their nerve endings to indulge me, maybe even romance me. I was speechless, delighted, and very much in the moment.

George set the tray on the floor in front of the hearth and got to work. First, he set up a Sterno can, then put the pot of thick, sweet-smelling fondue on a stand over the heat. The aroma was utterly decadent.

"Is it chocolate?" I marveled.

"The only thing in the world that's better: praline. Come on, sit down here."

Near the fondue pot he placed a plate loaded with purple grapes, red and green apple wedges, pecans and cashews, orange segments, and Oreos. Next to that, he set an ice bucket with two bottles of bubbly water. I joined him on the floor, and he handed me a cashew. "Watch your fingers—it's pretty hot," he said.

I dipped the nut into the pot. It was ambrosial, the creamy, butterscotchy fondue against the salty, crunchy nut. I still couldn't believe George was doing this all for me, for *me*.

At first, we were so busy talking—school, music, even astrology—we hardly ate. When George wanted to know what my favorite planet was, I was tempted to answer Venus but opted for the more demure Saturn. Later, remembering my first conversation with Rita, I asked George who he'd invite to a fantasy dinner party. He liked this question and conjured up a long list of icons, including Mick Jagger, Julia Child and Lucille Ball.

"Lucille Ball?"

"She was the funniest. You've got to laugh at a dinner party, or the food doesn't taste any good."

At one point, he sank an Oreo halfway into the praline and brought it to my lips. Then, right when I opened my mouth to receive it, he stole it back.

"Hey," I protested.

He put the plain half in his mouth and leaned toward me. I knew what he wanted me to do. I took the dipped half between my lips. It was a chocolate and praline kiss, ending only when the Oreo disintegrated on our tongues.

After that, we fed each other fondue cookies and fruit, not saying a word—not out loud, anyway. It was luscious and sticky and superbly messy. Most of all, it was enticing, George with his blue-green eyes and his praline lips, his gooey fingers and his beautiful smile. He ignited all my senses, until I was dizzy with the commotion inside me.

"Did you like it?" he asked when we ate the last Oreo. He brushed a stray crumb from my mouth, then licked it unhurriedly off his finger.

"Mmmm." We kissed again, until our mouths were almost glued together with praline. God, it felt good. "Maybe the couch would be more…"

"Good idea." He was kissing my ear now.

It was hard to pull away, but I forced myself to stand up, and he followed me to the couch. Sitting back, our arms and legs entwined, the moment felt perfect. There was no need to talk or move. It was enough, more than enough, to stretch out and watch the fire. The flames shimmied and swayed, making delicate shadow dances around us, their fluid moves reminding me of something, though I didn't know what. I lay my head on George's shoulder.

"Where are you?" George asked after a while.

"Hmm? Oh, I was just remembering the dream I had last night. About you."

"Did it involve whipped cream?"

"No, we were dancing. I was all dressed up and you were barely dressed—just swim trunks and sunglasses. They were playing 'Heat Wave.' Think it means something?"

"Uh huh—that you think about me even in your sleep." He tightened his legs around mine. "I had a dream about you too. Only, I was awake."

My insides swam, then stormed. "Tell me."

"I'd rather show you," he said, lacing his fingers with mine. His eyes were ocean tones, his skin glowing in stripes of shadow and light. Everything about him was heat, color and spice. I thought of deserts and tigers and chili peppers—and his sweet, sweet lips.

We slid down until we were lying on the couch. I was on my back, George's hands cradling my head, his pelvis resting lightly on mine. When he pressed his hips down, all the electricity in the universe leapt out of the skies into my body. I'd never felt like this, never imagined it possible, not for me. George sent me into such overdrive, I thought I might never sleep again. Like Dr. Seuss said, you know you're in love when you can't fall asleep because reality is finally better than your dreams.

Oh God, I was in love! One week may be an awfully short time to truly fall in love, but I had, completely. Whether George was in love or just in lust, I still had no clue, but there was still time to find out...wasn't there?

If only time could have paused just then. If only we could have tunneled through some cosmic wormhole where we could spend eons together—and then pop back out onto the couch without having lost a moment of real time. Suddenly two weeks at the Black Butterfly wasn't nearly long enough. I held him tighter. He lifted his lips to my ear and whispered, "Let's go to my room."

George's room was in the attic, at the end of a narrow corridor and kitty-corner to Bubbles' room. The small bedroom appeared flash frozen sometime circa George's seventh-grade year: the bed with the plaid comforter, the Coldplay poster taped to the wall, the student's desk piled with CDs and *Sports Illustrated*. We were barely inside when a loud clapping noise made me jump, but it turned out just to be his desk clock clicking from 11:59 to midnight and from December 23 to 24.

"Relax," he said, taking my hand.

"Sorry, it's just...wow, it's Christmas Eve already."

"Guess so. By the way, we don't do Christmas around here the way most families do."

"Meaning?"

"Well, for starters, we don't do gifts, not like normal people anyway. We pick names, and we give something we already own. Or that we make. But even then we're supposed to use stuff we have lying around. It's Ma's answer to the commercialization of Christmas, something like that."

That was a cool concept, I thought, especially since it got me off the gift hook. Presents were the last thing on my mind lately. "Whose name did you get?" I asked.

"Vincent. He likes gadgets, so I'm giving him my magnifying glass." He nodded toward the desk, where an antique-looking magnifying glass sat on one of the magazine stacks. It was a circle of thick glass set in a heavy silver frame, with a carved wooden handle. Very sturdy looking.

"I bet he'll love it."

George was about to say something when there was a rap at the door followed by Bubbles calling, "Georgie, do you have your financial aid papers handy?"

Jarred, I quickly retreated a few steps.

"C'mon in, Ma," he called back, although Bubbles already had the door halfway opened.

Clearly flustered to see that George wasn't alone, Bubbles looked at me while talking to him. "I'm sorry to interrupt." She looked kind of sad, and I somehow felt sorry for her. Her little boy had a girl in his room. "I—it can wait."

"No, no, we're totally interruptible," I said. "George was just showing me his..." My eye caught the stack of CDs on his desk. "...his music. We both like Bob Dylan."

"Well, I'm glad to see you kids have something in common." Unless it was my imagination, she emphasized the *kids* part.

"What are you doing up so late, Ma?" George asked.

"Couldn't sleep. Figured as long as I'm awake, I might as well do something productive. Besides, there's nothing on TV."

George dug some papers out of his backpack, which lay at the foot of the bed. "Here you go. I already filled in the work-study section."

"Thanks, sweetie." Her eyes drifted from him to me and back to him, crestfallen. "I guess I'll be going then. Georgie, remember, you're taking me to the mainland bright and early tomorrow. I've got to replace those crumbling wreaths before it's too late. We need more holly for the mantels too."

Must be nice when your biggest problems are the kind that can be solved by Martha Stewart. "Yeah, I'd better be going too," I said. What else could I do with Bubbles standing there, looking like we'd just sent her off on an ice floe to die? I desperately wanted to stay with George—for all kinds of reasons—but if I did, all I'd see would be her pitiful expression.

"All right then," Bubbles effervesced. "I'll walk you to your room, how's that?"

I smiled a reluctant smile at George, who shrugged and smiled back, and then Bubbles and I hit the stairs. She deposited me at my door and told me to get myself some P&Q. P&Q—around here? Like *that* was ever going to happen.

Chapter 9

I want to get away,
I want to fly away.
—*Lenny Kravitz, "Fly Away"*

I got up absurdly late the next morning, but I was still exhausted.
And wired. It was a dark-circles-under-the-eyes kind of day
if there ever was one. Taking a long hot shower didn't fix me
either, although it did help a little. I dried off, layered on my
warmest clothes, and realized I had no desire to venture out of
the room. Locked inside here, I felt safe from Starla.

God, I was pathetic. And hungry. My mind might be telling
me to stay inside my lilac cocoon, but my stomach was sending
me downstairs. I listened to my belly.

I picked a good afternoon to hang out with Rita in the
kitchen: besides her usual baking ingredients—sugar, eggs,
whipping cream—she had out a mess of chocolate blocks, as
well as bottles of dark rum, brandy and Kahlua, plus all kinds
of spices and extracts. She was making tiramisu eggnog trifle
for tonight's dessert and was now standing at the island, doing
something with a paintbrush.

Taking a stool, I helped myself to a square of chocolate.
This was exactly what I was in the mood for: comfort food. I
polished off my square and started a second one as I watched

Rita brush melted chocolate on the veined undersides of real lemon leaves. "What exactly are you doing?" I finally asked.

"Making chocolate leaves for garnish. We will chill these for a while, and then we can peel off the green-leaf backing. In Montreal, we brushed the chocolate leaves with real gold dust, but here I have none." She reached for a goblet sitting behind the sugar jar and swirled it before taking a sip.

"Brandy?" I asked.

"A little of everything."

I popped the last bit of chocolate into my mouth and licked my fingers, the way I usually only do when I'm by myself.

"My mother had a way to break that habit," Rita said, setting down her glass.

"What habit?"

"Using your tongue to wash your hands. If Maman caught you, you would have to wear mittens to your meals for the rest of the day."

I dropped my hands and wiped them on my jeans.

"Now, now," Rita said. "I did not say Maman was right. She had far too many rules for my liking. Go ahead, eat it however you like. Just save me enough chocolate to finish the leaves."

"Maybe I should help you," I suggested, although the job looked pretty involved.

Rita waved her painting brush in the air. "Not at all. I am just happy for the company. Besides, I am finished."

As I looked around for a napkin, the kitchen door swung open and George walked in wearing a heavy jacket and rosy cheeks. "There you are," he smiled. "Rita, you've been hiding her."

"Guilty as charged." She carried the tray of cooling

chocolate leaves to the fridge, making room between the cheeses and pickles. "Now, you will excuse me, yes? Penny, I am counting on you," she said from the doorway. "Do not let him touch that tray."

As soon as we were alone, he walked over and kissed me. "Mmm, I taste chocolate," he said.

"Gluttony is my sin. That and lust."

"My kind of girl," he said, pulling me into his pillows of down. "Hey, Vincent's going to drop me off at the barber's on his way to do some errands. You feel like getting out of the house for a while? You might have fun doing the rounds with Vincent."

Out of the house. Out of Starla's lair. A few minutes of respite. "Sounds great," I said.

Ten minutes after we piled into the van, George was getting his haircut at Shears, and Vincent and I were pulling into Darleen's Delectables—the lean-to off of old-timer Darleen Crocker's bungalow, next to the school building. The shop was both kitchen and store in one room, which made it cramped but also made it smell like I'd died and gone to brown sugar and butter heaven. Darleen herself was a compact, white-haired woman in overalls and reading glasses. When we walked in, she was piping pink frosting onto a cupcake while a large grey cat sat on the counter, watching curiously.

"Well, if it isn't Vincent Aylesworth," she said, coming around the counter to hug him.

"Hey, Darleen," he said. "You look lovely as ever."

"Right back atcha. Thank goodness Rita gets Christmas Day off, or we might never see each other, eh?"

"You kidding? I'd always come to see you."

"Good man. Say, who's your girlfriend?"

"This young lady is Penny, our special guest. Penny, this is Darleen, Islemorow's baker extraordinaire."

"Watch out, Penny—he'll twist you right around his pinky with that sweet-talk, mark my words. Now hold on, I've got your goodies all set." She returned to the counter—either unaware or unfazed that her cat was licking the cupcake she'd been frosting—and gathered up three large boxes labeled Henion. "Here we go."

"Got any Christmas Day muffins in here?" Vincent asked as he took the boxes from her.

"All the usual suspects. And plenty of them."

"Good woman."

It went on like that for a while—the chitchatting, the ringing up, the paying. Then we said our goodbyes, and Vincent and I were on our way. As we pulled back onto the road, I wondered if there was something mildly flirty to the banter I'd just witnessed. Darleen sure seemed happy to see Vincent, and he clearly wasn't in any rush to leave her shop. Maybe they had history together, or maybe they wanted to make history together. Then again, maybe they were just friendly island old-timers. Hell, for all I knew, there was a Mr. Delectable inside that bungalow. I would probably never find out.

After a few minutes, Vincent turned onto a narrow, barren street—a street, I couldn't avoid noticing, that teetered between two supremely deep ravines. "Next stop, old man Bigelow's," he said.

"Who?" I asked, looking out my window and down, down, down to the ground below. The road was barely as wide as the van.

"Jimmy Bigelow. Best woodworker on the island. He just refinished an old rocking chair for me. Won't take but a jiffy to pick her up."

My eyes were glued to the zigzag path and the steep drops on either side of us. "You sure this is safe, Vincent?"

"Sure what's safe?"

"This road."

"Course. Why, you afraid of heights?"

"Not usually..."

"I used to be. The trick is to keep looking straight forward, not down."

I pulled my eyes off the rocky crags and focused on the road ahead. He was right—it did help, a little. It also helped when Vincent started belting out "Winter Wonderland" in a key that only a tone deaf baritone could achieve. He misunderstood the lyrics too, singing, "Later on, we'll count spiders, as we drink by the fire, to face, I'm afraid, the plans that we made, walking in a winter wonderland." Or maybe he was doing it all on purpose.

"Almost there," Vincent said. "Jimmy works out of his garage, did I say? A non-commuter type, just like me." Then he began crooning about Frosty the Snowman's "corncob pipe and bloody nose and two eyes made out of sole."

I was about to suggest that perhaps it was a button nose, but something else caught my attention. Something behind me. Movement. A slight, wispy sound. A draft. I glanced in the rearview mirror.

It was Starla. She must have been in the van the whole time! *Oh, God, now what?*

She was climbing from the trunk to the backseat. One leg up and over, then the other, until she fell into the seat with an airy laugh. "Hello, Penny," she said. "I haven't been out riding in a while. This is a treat."

I didn't speak or even turn around, but I'm sure she sensed my panic.

She leaned forward and laid her hand lazily on Vincent's shoulder. "Tell me now, what brings the two of you out on a wintry day like this?"

"Vincent," I said, my throat burning. "I...you need to stop."

"Stop what?"

"The van. Something's wrong."

"I'm telling you, Penny, it's just a bumpy road, that's all. We're fine."

"No, we're not." As I said this, Starla was on the move again, climbing from the backseat straight onto Vincent's lap, where she put one hand on the steering wheel. "Don't!" I said without thinking. "I mean, sorry, Vincent...I just really think... would you please..."

We came to a sharp curve in the path. The ravines on either side of us were menacingly deep. "Vincent, please—"

"Get ready now," Starla said. "This is where the ride gets fun. This is where you have a terrible accident." She gripped the steering wheel with both hands now. "To the left, I think, don't you?"

"Stop!" I shouted. I grabbed the wheel and yanked hard to the right. "Stop it!"

Vincent slammed on the brakes and tried to straighten the wheel. We skidded. Fishtailed. Kept on moving, no matter how hard he pumped the brakes. Kept going straight ahead, even as the road twisted. Within seconds, our front end slid off the road and dipped down toward the ravine. We halted just before the back wheels went over the edge.

"Christ!" Vincent said, gunning it in reverse. The two rear wheels had to do all the work, and they didn't like it. They spun and buzzed and screeched before finally pulling the rest of the van back onto the path. The front fender hit the dirt with a clunk.

"Oh dear," Starla said with counterfeit concern. "Not exactly the results I was hoping for. Too bad."

Vincent and I sat there stupefied for what must have been a full minute before either of us spoke. "What the hell was that about?" he asked, pulling the emergency brake. "You could have gotten us killed."

Oh God, he thought it was all my doing—that I grabbed the wheel for no reason and drove us off the road! "Vincent," I started, but he was already stepping out of the van to check for damage. Starla got out with him.

"Bye, Penny," she chirped. "I'm going to walk the rest of the way. See you at home." She sauntered along the curve in the road, quickly disappearing from sight.

"Seems okay," Vincent said when he got back in. "Fender's dinged a little, that's all. Thank heaven for all-wheel drive."

I dropped my head against the headrest and blew out a lungful of air. "I'm so sorry, Vincent. I don't know what I was thinking. I guess..."

"Never mind. Just, no more touching the steering wheel, all right?"

I nodded, and we drove the rest of the way to Jimmy Bigelow's in silence.

🦋

Yes, I'm the great pretender
Pretending that I'm doing well
—The Platters

When we got back to the inn, Bubbles was standing in the doorway waiting for us. "George, Penny," she gushed. "It's Christmas Eve—do let's spend it together!" With those words, my plan to run straight upstairs evaporated. All I wanted was to find Blue, tell him what happened, and fall apart in peace, but instead I had to suck it up and pretend to be in the holiday mood. I wasn't sure I was strong enough—or good enough an actor—to get through the evening intact.

The three of us sat at Bubbles' favorite table for supper— minted lamb and mushroom kebabs, asparagus with walnut dressing, roasted pepper salad, and bread made from filo dough. Too bad I had zero appetite, not even for that amazing-looking tiramisu eggnog trifle at the end. Instead, I played with my food, cutting it and rearranging it on the plate to create the appearance of eating.

A two-hour meal didn't get me off the hook either. After dessert, Bubbles wanted to finish her (third) glass of wine in the study, so off we went, piling onto the sofa, Bubbles in the middle, to watch the tail end of *A Christmas Story*. Of course, once we were settled there, Bubbles insisted we stay on for *Miracle on 34th Street*, which reduced her to tears when everyone believed in Santa Claus at the end.

"Mercy, it's almost midnight already," she said when the commercials came on after *Miracle*. "We should all get some sleep. Tomorrow's a big day, after all." She got up off the couch and strolled to the doorway. "Night now, you two."

"Finally," George said, scooting over and wrapping his arm around me.

I put my head on his shoulder and faked a yawn. "Wow, I'm zonked all of a sudden. Today was my first time out since…the accident. I think it's hitting me."

"You feeling okay?" he asked, massaging my arm.

"Yeah, fine, just really sleepy. I think I better call it a day."

"I'll walk you up."

Just then Bubbles reappeared in the doorway, swaying slightly, looking happy and a little confused. "Why don't you walk your mom up instead?" I suggested. "She looks like she could use the help."

🦋

The truth is more important than the facts.
—Frank Lloyd Wright

As soon as Bubbles and George were gone, I ran upstairs to the Foxglove Room. "Blue?" I whispered, hoping no people were in earshot. "Blue, let me in. I need to talk."

I heard footsteps move quickly across the carpet and a hand grab the knob. The door opened, and Blue appeared, looking worried. "Penny, what's wrong?"

"Everything. I was out—"

"Come in. We shouldn't talk in the hall."

The Foxglove Room was similar to the Lilac Room, except

that it was navy blue instead of lavender, it had armchairs instead of loveseats, and there was a mirror instead of a print hanging above the mantel. Blue sat down on the bed and motioned me to join him.

"She almost killed me. Again," I said.

Blue's face darkened.

"Vincent too this time. While we were out in the van."

He closed his eyes and took a shallow breath. "I never should have let it go this far in the first place."

I wished more than anything that I could put my hand on his cheek and that he could take comfort from my touch. But I couldn't. He couldn't. We couldn't.

"She's won, Penny. You must know that. I'm going to give her what she wants and stay away from you."

"What? No! No way."

"It's not worth your life," he said.

"Yeah, but she'll keep trying to kill me anyway. Even if we never talk again. Because she doesn't want me around George either."

Blue's eyes widened. "You think she loves George too?"

"Yes, but not in the way you're thinking. George is her son, Blue. He's the person she's waiting for."

Blue's mouth opened a sliver. "Why do you think that?"

"My dream journey. It was all there."

"Penny, I told you, dream journeys aren't always factual, not in a literal way."

"I know, but I know this one is true. It fits with what George has told me. And besides, it felt real—literally, factually real."

"I don't know," he said.

"Have you noticed how careful she's been to spare George in these so-called accidents? How she lured me to the dock only after George was safely out of bounds? How she didn't pull the car stunt when George was on board? She doesn't want to murder her own son. She just wants to keep him from getting involved with a girl who can see her prowling around."

Blue shook his head.

"Don't you see?" I said. "Starla will have it in for me even if you drop me. So there's no reason for us to stop...hanging out."

His eyes seared mine with that incredible flame from behind. After a long minute he said, "I need some time to think. Can you give me that?"

Panic rose in my throat. "But—"

"Please," he said softly. "I need to be alone."

Unable to speak, I stood up, went to the door, and walked grimly out of the room.

Chapter 10
December 25

I know the answer! The answer lies within the heart of all mankind! The answer is twelve? I think I'm in the wrong building.
—Charles M. Schulz

Another sleepless night. Sleepless, terrified, heartbroken, furious. Was Starla already hatching her next plot against me? Was Blue truly going to shut me out? Was he telling Starla as much right now—and was she trying to get all toasty with him this very minute? God, she made me sick.

Between tossings and turnings, I had the on-and-off urge to call Mom. I felt an overwhelming impulse to confess everything I now knew to be true about ghosts. *Don't do it*, I warned myself repeatedly. *Don't tangle Mom up in your odyssey. Don't tangle yourself up in Mom's mania.* But it would be so easy to tell her, and such a relief. *No. No, no, no.* But what if she called tomorrow, for Christmas? Would I be able to resist the opening?

As the night wore on, I started obsessing about George and me. He seemed smitten now. He was acting chivalrous now. But what would happen once we parted—once he was back in college, surrounded by girls, living in a different state from me? Would I still be worth the hassle? Or would I be out of sight and out of mind? The thought of losing both him and Blue was like a taste of death.

I finally gave up on the idea of ever falling asleep. Sitting up in bed, I watched the world outside my window turn from black to charcoal, and from purplish silver to steely grey. When the snow started to look white instead of slate, I decided morning had arrived. Christmas Day. The day to be merry, or at least to act merry.

The idea of playing Perky Penny made me so tired I lay back down for half an hour. I probably would have stayed horizontal longer, but suddenly Alvin and the Chipmunks were downstairs singing "Christmas Don't Be Late" at the top of their rodent lungs, so I dragged myself out of bed, changed into my red snowflake sweater and good jeans, ran a brush through my hair and my teeth, and headed downstairs.

"Penny dear, good morning," Bubbles said in her consummate hostess voice when I arrived in the parlor. "Welcome to Christmas at the Black Butterfly."

George, Rita and Vincent walked in from the direction of the kitchen, carrying trays of Darleen's Delectables, which they set on the coffee table next to several pitchers of juice. Then we all wished each other happy holidays and started filling our plates. George touched my hand as he passed me a juice glass, and my feelings for him swelled to overflowing. It was such a warm, reassuring touch, I wanted to bottle it and keep it with me always.

Once we sat down, Bubbles did most of the talking— surprise, surprise—which was fine by me and, I think, by the others. I nodded and smiled at her when it seemed appropriate, and kept my mouth shut when it didn't. Finally she drained her glass of orange juice (or maybe it was a mimosa), blotted her crimson lips, and announced, "All right, shall we get to the goodies?" Everyone except me went to the tree and retrieved the newspaper-and-foil-wrapped packages they were about to exchange.

This year, it turned out, Bubbles had drawn George's name, and she was obviously thrilled to pass on a jade and crystal chess set to him. George gave Vincent the magnifying glass. Rita presented Bubbles with a pewter moose, and Vincent gave Rita a poster of every kind of mushroom.

"Did I not give you this poster a few Christmases ago?" Rita asked Vincent playfully.

"Yes," he said, "and I'm looking forward to getting it back the next time you draw my name."

I thought the gift-giving portion of the morning was complete, but then Rita said, "I have a little something for Penny, as well." She took a bag out from behind her. "Just a very little something." I took the bag and pulled out *A Pictorial History of Chocolate*, a colorful, oversized book complete with recipes and maps. I hugged Rita tightly, thinking as I did how much more thoughtful she was than my own mother sometimes.

Bubbles pressed a small box into my hand. "I have something for you too, dear," she said. It took me a little while to open the box, which was not only wrapped but also tied with all kinds of yarn and ribbons. Inside was a pin, the kind you'd wear on a blazer or denim jacket, shaped like a chameleon and glimmering different colors depending on how the light hit it. The eyes were glass, the tail was wire, and the body was a hodgepodge of computer circuitry.

"I love it," I told her. And I honestly did sort of like it.

"I suppose it's my turn now," Vincent said. He handed me a worn paperback copy of Stephen King's *Misery*.

"Vincent, this is perfect," I said, although I'd already read the book twice and seen the movie a bunch of times. "Thank you, everyone, so much. This is an awesome Christmas."

I caught sight of Starla just as I set my gifts on the coffee table. She was standing at the bottom of the staircase, hands behind her back, watching us. God, I wanted to strangle her. I wanted to grab her by the throat and make her tell me where Blue was, make her promise to leave me alone, make her go the hell away. I couldn't, of course. I could only stare back at her, which made me even more furious. The girl who wanted to ruin—or end—my life was in the room, and all I could do was keep smiling.

As I eyed Starla, I realized there was something different about her. Something about her face, something subtle but definitely there. It took me a second to figure it out. Then it hit me. The hostility was still in her eyes, but it was mixed with something else, something like…longing. Like she was a little girl with her nose pressed against a toy store window after closing time. Locked out. I might actually have felt sorry for her if she weren't such a diabolical bitch.

Rita was the only one who sensed my distress. She was suddenly at my side, her arm around my waist. "Penny, are you okay?" she asked, which got George up off the couch and headed my way. Bubbles got there before him though, and she took my hand and asked if I felt faint.

I tore my eyes away from Starla. "No, no, I'm fine. Sorry. It's nothing. I'm just…I just figured out what I'd've given you all if I'd been organized." I glanced up in time to see Starla running up the stairs. *Steady, Penny. Stay focused. Think.* "Fortune cookies. Homemade fortune cookies with a personalized message inside. A quote."

"Sounds like fun," Bubbles said, walking me over to the couch. "Want to try it now? Not the cookie—just the quote."

Like I had a choice. "Okay, I guess I can give it a shot. Give me a minute…Vincent, you first. *Smell is a potent wizard that transports you across thousands of miles and all the years you have lived.* That's from Helen Keller."

He blinked vacantly at me, and I thought I was going to have to remind him how he sniffed out my first supper here, but then a smile of recognition crept over his face.

"Bubbles, let's see. *Forgiveness doesn't change the past, but it does enlarge the future.* I can't remember who said it, but, well, anyway."

She blew me a kiss with her ruby-lipsticked lips and her scarlet-nailed hand, and I think her cheeks went a little red, as well.

"Rita, this one's from Toni Morrison. *She is a friend of my mind…the pieces I am, she gathers them and gives them back to me in all the right order.*"

Rita was just starting to say something when the lobby phone rang. "I'll get it," she said.

"No, I'll get it," said George, which was a good thing because I had no idea what quote to give him, especially in front of his mother. He breezed back in a minute later and handed me the phone. "Your mother."

So Mom thought of me on Christmas, after all.

"Hey, Mom," I said. "Can I call you back in just a bit? We're in the middle of—"

"Sorry, honey, but I won't be near a phone later," she said. "It's important. Maybe you should take the phone somewhere you can be alone."

It's always useful to know where a friend and relation is, whether you want him or whether you don't.

—*Rabbit,* POOH'S LITTLE INSTRUCTION BOOK

I plopped onto the cyclone of bedcovers and lit the Tiffany lamp. "Okay, all set, Mom. Shoot."

"First of all, Merry Christmas. How *is* it having Christmas in Maine? Got snow?"

"Snow, ice, wind—you name it, we've got it."

"It's cold here too."

"Where are you calling from? It's a good connection for once."

"Yes, finally. It's so great to hear your voice. I can't wait to see you and give you your present. I got you something special out here. I hope you're okay with not having gifts to open today. It's just that I didn't—"

"I did have gifts to open."

"Really? From Bubbles? Bubbles got you a Christmas present?"

"Yes. Bubbles and my other friends here."

"You have friends there? That's terrific, honey. This time, we're both having an adventure, huh?"

"You could say that."

She didn't say anything for a moment, and I was beginning to think our connection was breaking up, but then I detected an unmistakable sound, the sound of a warning breath rocketing straight from the Rocky Mountains to my ears. All my senses sharpened, and I unconsciously pulled my knees up to my chest.

"Mom, you there?"

"Right here, sweetie."

"You said you had something important to tell me."

"Yes, something exciting. Are you sitting down?"

I clasped the comforter. "Uh huh."

"Okay," she said, drawing the word out into several syllables. "Remember when I told you I was going to interview the owner of the Shotgun Murder Mansion? His name is Rex. It was the last time we spoke."

"I remember."

"Well, I did it, and I got it on tape. One of the best pieces I've ever done. He was a great interview—funny and knowledgeable, and the camera liked him too."

"Don't tell me you sold it."

"Better than that. Rex offered me a job! Isn't that wonderful? Giving tours at the mansion—it's a museum now. And doing research. Oh, and getting publicity for the museum. Salary, benefits, three weeks vacation. A real professional job in my chosen field. I'm so excited. I start in two weeks."

"What?" A job in Coyote, Idaho, a.k.a. the middle of nowhere. A world away from everything I know. A universe away from George. Two weeks from now. I dropped back onto the headboard and banged my head. *No, no, no.*

"Penny, are you still there?"

"Uh."

"Well, isn't it incredible? This could be a whole new life

for both of us. It *will* be a new life. A better life. Without all the moving and scrimping and mooching off friends. Don't you see?"

I saw all right. I saw how Mom got what Mom wanted, and she didn't care that it was going to ruin my life. Care? She never even thought about it. She never once stopped to wonder how I might feel. Because my feelings, my whole life, didn't matter.

"Penny, say something."

Corralling every drop of self-control I had, I took a deep, cleansing breath. "Look, Mom, there are real jobs in Boston too."

"Not like this one. This is the job I've been holding out for."

"We don't *have* to move all the time or mooch off Gigi. We've never *had* to. It's been your choice."

"Penny." Her voice climbed an octave. "I made those choices with you in mind, for you."

This made me laugh. "So you think I like living the way we do? You think I like having a new address and a new school every time I turn around? No, Mom. I do it because you make me, that's why."

"I make you because that's how I keep a roof over your head," she said, her words shaking a little. "But from now on, it doesn't have to be that way. Now we'll have one address, one school. There's a nice little Catholic school —"

"Catholic school!"

"Now honey, it's just that Coyote is so small and out of the way, it doesn't have much of a school system. Over in Ketchum—that's about two hours from here—they have a Catholic boarding school for girls, and it's supposed to be—"

"Boarding school? Why don't you just ship me off to

Timbuktu while you're at it? Then I'll really be out of your hair. That's what you want, isn't it?"

"Penny, it's not like that at all. I just want you to go to a good school, now that I'll be able to afford one. You'll come home every weekend, of course. And over the summer, I have an idea about taking a family vacation."

"Family vacation—ha. We don't take vacations, Mom. *You* take vacations, and you leave me with whoever will take me."

"Not anymore."

I barely heard her. I was on the rampage. "Why did you wait until today to drop the bomb on me? Is this your so-called special Christmas present?"

I could hear her breathing fast, as if she were running after the right thing to say. "I only got the job offer today."

"Someone made you a job offer on Christmas Day? Where are you anyway? You never told me where you are."

"I know," she said, sounding a little cheerier now. "I'm at Rex's house. That's why the connection is good—I'm on his landline. He and I hit it off so well at the interview, we've been spending time together. We like each other, Penny. More than like. We're in love."

The phone dropped out of my hand and rolled off the pillow. I spent a long, otherworldly moment staring at the ceiling, watching my life flash before my eyes. Not my life-to-date, like people claim they see just before the oncoming truck hits their windshield. More like my future life, the one that just got pulled out from under me, the one that involved, among other things, George. Mom had a whim and poof! I was going to be living at a Catholic boarding school in Idaho.

"Penny?" she said as I picked the receiver back up.

"Mom, you don't even know this guy. What if it doesn't work out between you? Then what will happen to your job, to us? What if he doesn't like me? Then we'd be stuck out there with nothing."

"But I do know him. Look, I know this is sudden, but…hey, remember the *Parent Trap*, how the parents meet on a cruise and get married before they reach shore? True love can happen that fast."

"Yeah, and what about the part where they spend the next decade on different continents?"

"It has a happy ending though, doesn't it? Look, Penny, Rex is perfect for me. My soul mate. And he's going to adore you. We're going to be happy, I just know it. All five of us."

"Five?"

"He has twin sons, Liam and Jared. They go to the boys' boarding school just across the way from the girls'."

Was the entire universe colluding to play a big fat cosmic joke on me, making every possible disaster turn into a reality? It sure as hell seemed that way. I didn't want to ask any more questions because I was afraid to learn the answers, yet I had to know. "Mom, are you planning on having us move in with this guy Rex?"

"He's got a beautiful place, honey. A house, a real honest-to-goodness house. And spacious. You'll have your own bedroom and bathroom, and there's a hot tub off the back deck, and I'll tell you, his TV is bigger than some of the apartments we've had. So don't you go worrying about the living arrangements. It's all taken care of."

She's flipped. My mother's precarious sanity has left the building. She's fallen in love with a stranger, she's pulling up every stake, and she's taking me down with her. Nothing could be more obvious. Or more horrifying.

"Penny, did you hear the part about having your own shower? And that family vacation I mentioned? Rex has an RV that can fit all five of us, and we can go anywhere we want."

A little spider on the ceiling caught my eye then. It reminded me of *Charlotte's Web*, of the motherly grey spider that must die right after laying her eggs. Salmon do the same thing. I learned that on a school field trip. And male praying mantises sacrifice their heads in the mating process. These creatures give up their lives for their children. My mother, on the other hand, wouldn't even give up her ludicrous fantasies for her offspring.

"I know it's a lot to take in now, all at once," I vaguely heard her say. "But you'll see. Once you get here, you'll see how right it is. I really love him, Penny."

Some French guy—I forgot his name—said there's always a little madness in love, but there's always a little reason in madness. I read it in one of the first murder mysteries I ever got at the Poison Pen. I hated that book.

"Mom, can't you two just, I don't know, take it a little slower? What's the rush after all these years alone?"

She sighed and cleared her throat. "I know, honey, I know. The thing is, well, there are a couple of things. One is, the job opening won't wait. If I don't take the offer now, it'll have to go to someone else, and then what would I do for work around here? The other thing is, I just know we're meant to be together. As a family. All of us."

"But Mom—"

"I'm taking the red-eye back tonight to start packing up, and you should come home now too. I booked you on the last flight out of Machias tomorrow…wait a minute, honey, hold on." A sound like ripping paper came through the phone. "Sweetie, I didn't realize, we're running late for church, so—"

"Since when do you go to church?"

"It *is* Christmas Day," she said. Rex must have been listening in.

"I repeat, since when do you go to church? Or is this part of the new you? The big-house-with-the-white-picket-fence-and-a-regular-job you."

"And what's wrong with that?" She was angry now. "Didn't you just say you don't like the old me?"

"I never said that. Don't put words in my mouth, Mom."

"Okay, fine. Look, the boys are already in the car. I'm going to have to say goodbye now, but your flight number is 712, and it leaves from Machias at, hold on, 12:18 tomorrow. You'll have to take the T back to Cambridge." Then her voice became softer. "Penny, try to understand, won't you? Please, try to understand."

I would never understand. Instead, I fell back on my pillow and willed myself into the place where I didn't have to think or feel or know or wonder or worry. As I closed the curtain around my awful world, the pillowcase grew damp with my tears.

Chapter 11

Love is a verb here in my room.
—Incubus, "Here in my Room"

George had to pound on my door to rouse me. I huddled there
under the covers trying to figure out who I was and what year it
was, and when the truth found its way into my head, I wanted to go
back to not knowing. Turning away from the door, I nestled deeper
under the sheets. But George kept banging. "Penny, it's me."

"Come in," I finally croaked, fumbling for the Tiffany lamp.
"It's locked."

"Oh, sorry." I got up, finger combing my hair and praying
that I looked better than I felt, and let him in.

"Sorry I woke you. I just, I got worried."

"How long have I been up here?" I asked, sitting cross-
legged on the bed.

"Close to two hours." He kicked off his sneakers and joined
me. "So...how are you?"

I really didn't want to talk about it, not even to George.
Talking about it meant thinking about it, and thinking about
it meant feeling miserable, and feeling miserable meant I was
awake, and all I wanted was to be asleep. Asleep and oblivious.

"You're a sound sleeper," he said. "For a minute I thought I
was gonna have to call the fire department to axe down the door."

"Don't laugh. When I was eight, someone had a kitchen

fire in our building. Mom was working late, and I slept right through the alarms and the sirens, right there on the living room couch with the TV blaring."

George's eyebrows crept together. "Wasn't someone staying with you, a babysitter or something?"

"Nope. We didn't have any free sitters in that place, so if Mom had to work nights, I just stayed up watching reruns until I fell asleep in front of the tube. Here, I'll prove it. Quiz me on any *ER* or *X-Files* episode—I've seen them all a zillion times."

He didn't see the humor here, which I guess made sense since there wasn't any. "That sucks. Anyway, are you okay? You aren't sick, are you?"

Such short, simple questions. Such long, complicated answers. His hand was warm and sturdy, the one piece of real life I was glad to hold onto. "No, not sick." I didn't want to ruin this moment by dragging reality into it, so I didn't offer any other explanation.

He scooted closer and lowered his voice. "And your mom?"

"What about her?"

"She called right before you came upstairs, remember? How is she?"

"She's fine. Perfect. Delightful." Then the tears came.

He uncrossed his legs and pulled me to his chest. "I'm sorry," he said.

"She was informing me that we're moving to Idaho. Immediately. She thinks she's in love, and she's moving us in with some guy and his kids. I have to fly back to Boston tomorrow afternoon."

George's mouth unclasped. He didn't say anything at first.

Then, in a soft, incredulous voice, "Idaho? But I thought we'd be able to…"

"Me too. Idaho—Jesus. I've lived with Mom's bullshit for sixteen years, and even I can't believe she'd pull something like this." I fell supine on the bed.

"Not exactly the Christmas greeting you were expecting."

"Someday I'll learn to stop expecting anything from her. Anything good, that is."

At this, George's eyes narrowed into slits, and he brought two fingers to his lips. After a pensive moment he said, "I guess now's the time."

"Time for what?"

He lay back on the bed with me. "Well, I was going to wait until New Year's Eve for this—I thought it would be, you know, romantic or something that way. But Penny," and here he smiled a shy, uncertain smile, "you're invited to stay with us for the summer."

"George?" I couldn't let myself believe what I was pretty sure he just said.

"I talked to Ma about it a couple of days ago. She thinks it's a great idea. Which it is."

"I-I don't understand. I mean, how could you afford to have me take up room during your busy season?"

"We'll work something out. Besides, it's not like you'll be getting a free ride. This is going to be my first season working in the kitchen as Rita's sous chef. I want you to work with me."

"A sous sous chef? But I don't know how to cook."

"You'll have great teachers."

I glanced at the Tiffany lamp glowing pink against the

lavender walls, just like a summer sunset. God, summer at the Black Butterfly. Cooking by day, kicking back by night, watching the upper crusty guests do their upper crusty thing. Seeing Rita and the others—and hopefully Blue—again. Best of all, being with George, knowing he wanted to be with me. What a sublime fantasy.

Except for the Starla factor. Could I survive a whole summer with her? I mean literally—could I stay alive? And was it fair to the other people who might get caught in the crossfire? Someone besides me could get hurt—it almost happened to Vincent already. George was probably the only one who was physically safe, but even he wasn't out of harm's way emotionally. If something happened to me, he'd find a way to blame himself, just like he did when I almost drowned. Starla was the one being who could take a summer of paradise and turn it into hell.

"God, it sounds wonderful," I said, but I could hear the apprehension outstripping the elation in my voice.

He took my hand. "What's wrong?"

"I, um, I'm just not ready to leave here yet. I really wanted to…I was hoping we'd…"

"Me too."

"And summer is so far away."

"Yeah, but we've got Skype and phones and email."

"And thousands of miles between us."

"And June to look forward to."

"If I can get Mom to buy in."

"Is there any reason to think she won't?"

"I don't know, she's already talking about taking a

Very Brady family vacation this summer. She's absolutely certifiable, but I'll work on her." Then, with more resolve, I added, "Whatever it takes."

We fell into silence then, George playing with my fingers, me trying to figure out where Mom's life went wrong. Did it go all the way back to the Mayan cave? Did The Donor do something to mess her up? Did I wreck her simply by being born? No, Mom's brand of insanity couldn't be blamed on a single event or person. It's like that saying: each snowflake in an avalanche pleads not guilty. You need a lot of flakes working together to produce a snowballing wad of lunacy like hers.

"Penny?" he said after a while.

"Mm hmm?"

"I was just wondering, when you were doing your virtual fortune cookies, did you think of a quote for me?"

"Why, you feeling left out?"

"Sort of."

For some reason, I reached over and touched the scar on his eyebrow. "As a matter of fact, I did. Here. *Are we going to be friends forever? asked Piglet. Even longer, Pooh answered.*"

He looked at me intently.

"Well," I asked, "what do you think?"

"I think you should know I'm way beyond friends."

That's when I understood what people mean when they say they melted. In that moment, my internal radiator surged. Everything solid inside—every bone, every organ, every inch of flesh—turned into molten desire. I hungered, ached, thirsted, itched and, yes, melted for George. If Starla killed me now, I'd die happy. "I'm glad," I said.

We talked for a long time after that—about the summer, about the long months until June, about silly things and important things. And then suddenly we weren't talking at all.

Yes, clothes came off. No, we didn't go all the way. Yes, it was glorious—intimate and somehow beyond physical. No, no one said the L word. And yes, we eventually drifted off to sleep, still wrapped around each other, skin against skin, heartbeat against heartbeat.

I used to be Snow White—but I drifted.
—Mae West

When I woke up, George's slow, rhythmic breathing told me he was still deeply asleep. I lay there for a while, rocked by the rise and fall of his chest. Then I gently untangled myself from his arms, pulled my clothes back on, and went to break the news of my departure to some of the others.

First stop was the Foxglove Room, but Blue wasn't there. He didn't answer when I called outside the Tiger Lily Room either. Was he just out for one of his walks, or was he trying to protect me from Starla by hiding from me? I couldn't leave without letting him know I'd be back in June. All I wanted was one last moment with him, just one. Would he really deny me that? "Damn you, Blue," I muttered as I headed up to the attic.

Bubbles had a doorknocker shaped like a Buddha. I rapped the handle against the Buddha's belly but got no answer, so I knocked louder. Finally I heard what sounded like bedsprings and then the padding of feet across a rug. Bubbles was putting an arm through her bathrobe sleeve as she opened the door, her red hair squashed down on one side.

"Oh Bubbles, I woke you."

"No worries, just catching a little snooze," she said, holding the door open wider. "Come in, dear. Is everything all right?"

I stepped into her room, which was larger and more stylish than George's. A queen-size brass bed angled out from one corner, and a curio filled with colorful glass eggs stood between the bed and the wall. Under the window, there was a marble dressing table, on top of which sat a mother-and-baby photo of Bubbles and George. A small pink sofa stood on the far side of the room, and we installed ourselves on it now.

"What's on your mind, dear? Something's troubling you, I think."

I was going to make the long story short, but I ended up spilling every detail I knew about Coyote and Rex and the ghost museum and leaving here tomorrow. It all came bursting out like a swarm of angry hornets. The facts, the feelings, the ranting.

Bubbles didn't say anything at first. She spent a minute fingering her chain necklace and using her toes to flip a slipper that had come loose. Finally she forced the edges of her mouth up and said, "My, my, isn't that exciting? Idaho. I do hear it's lovely out there. So Viv is really in love. That's just…just splendid." Her voice couldn't have sounded less convincing.

"Well, Mom thinks it's splendid. I think it's lunacy."

Bubbles put her arm around my shoulders. She smelled like the brandy Rita sometimes cooked with. "Come now, let's try to think of this as a fresh start. It could turn out to be the best thing that's ever happened to either one of you, for all you know."

"What I know is that this is a crazy decision, and the ten seconds she spent thinking it through didn't take me into account. I hate her, Bubbles." I felt foolish at my outburst, but not foolish enough to take any of it back.

Now she was pushing my hair behind my ear and hushing me, telling me I didn't mean that.

"Wanna bet?" I asked. "I'll die out there in Idaho."

"No, you won't. You are well loved. No one will let you fall."

For some reason, this made me feel even worse. "Why are you so nice to me?" I asked.

"What kind of question is that?"

I sat up straighter and pulled a Kleenex out of my pants pocket. After a good long blow, I said, "With what happened between you and my mother—honestly, I don't know why you ever agreed to take me in. I wouldn't have. I'd still be raging."

Bubbles looked bewildered. "Penny, dear, what exactly did your mother tell you about us?"

"My mother? You're in the wrong universe, Bubbles. My mother doesn't tell me anything. I found out through…" Had I promised Rita to keep this a secret? No. Would I get her in trouble if I confessed? Maybe.

"Through who?" she asked earnestly.

"It doesn't matter."

"Yes, it does."

I looked away.

"You've at least got to tell me what you know," she said.

"I know my mother thought there was a ghost here. That she made a huge deal of it. That George ended up getting hurt in the kitchen crawlspace. That in the end, she stormed off."

The Black Butterfly

Bubbles had the strangest response to this dredging up of the awful past: she suppressed a smile.

"What?" I demanded.

She patted my hand, her sparkly bracelet tinkling coolly against my skin. "I need a drink," she said, and then I saw that she had one already poured on her dressing table. She retrieved it and took a long swig as she sat back down. "Better. It's probably rude not to offer you anything, but I don't have anything soft up here."

"I'm all set." But of course, I wasn't all set and never would be.

Bubbles set her glass on the floor and curled her legs under her. "I'll tell you what I'm going to do for you, Penny. I'm going to set you straight."

I folded my arms. "What does that mean?"

"You've got it all wrong, my love."

"Are you trying to tell me she wasn't nosing around? Because I know she was."

"No, that part is true. Viv thought there was a ghost, and I nixed the—what did she call it?—the investigation, and we had words after George got injured. But the reason she left the next day is that she was scheduled to leave then, not because we weren't friends anymore."

"Wait a minute," I said. "You mean, you weren't mad at her?"

"For a day. Then I blew my spout and was over it. I'm pretty sure Viv was over it too. We had some laughs her last night here, and I took her to the ferry the next day. We parted with the promise that I'd visit her in Chicago before the end of the year."

"Oh come on, Bubbles." I felt overheated, so I took off

my sweatshirt and wiped my face on it. "If everything was fine between you and Mom, then how come you two never spoke again until last week?"

"But that's not true. We did talk. I kept my promise about visiting. I left George with Rita—he was just a toddler—and I flew out over the Columbus holiday." Her face tightened, and she closed her eyes for so long, I thought she was falling asleep. "That was quite a weekend."

"You mean, Mom did something rotten again?"

Bubbles' eyes dampened. With two fingers, she squeezed the bridge of her nose, as if it were an off-button for her tears. "No, Penny. *I* did something rotten."

"You? Miss Congeniality? What could you possibly do to offend anyone?"

"I could do plenty. I'm just not sure it's my place to tell you. If Viv didn't tell you herself, then—"

"Tell me," I said so forcefully, she visibly flinched. "Sorry. Sorry for shouting. But I need you to tell me. Please."

She looked around for something to do with her hands. All she came up with was tidying her out-of-joint hair. "I've never told a living soul about this. Lord, just the thought of it makes me nervous."

"It's only me. And I like you. I'm on your side. It's fine."

She eyed me uncertainly, took another sip of her drink, and exhaled loudly. Then she started talking to her slippers. "Okay, all right, here goes. Viv and Justin—that's your dad— were living together in this cute little apartment on Oak Street. It was my first time meeting him—it was my first time in Chicago—and your mom was all excited about it. She had a track record of dating men who were what you might call..." She bit her lip. "...inappropriate. She really wanted to show off Justin because she thought he was different from the others. Better. She'd been telling me how wonderful he was for months."

"What *was* he like?" I asked.

"Viv was telling the truth, Penny. I was only there for a short time, but I got to know him. See, your mom got called in to work that Sunday at the Pizza Hut—she was rip-roaring mad about it, but what could she do?—so Justin and I spent the whole day walking the city. He was smart and ambitious, and what he lacked in good looks, he made up for in humor. He was funny as heck, but never at anyone's expense. That's a gentleman, unlike some of Viv's previous boyfriends."

Bubbles seemed to be remembering something troublesome now. Her face constricted. Then she inhaled—a warning breath?—and asked, "Shall I continue?"

I nodded, feeling my own muscles tense up too.

"Viv's boss took pity on her and let her out a couple of hours early, on account of it being a slower day than expected. Okay, so here's the hard part..."

Hard for who? Her, Mom, me? Could hearing it—whatever *it* was—be that much harder to take than the anxiety of waiting for her to spit it out? "I'm listening," I urged.

"All right." She laughed anxiously, the air fluttering in her throat. "When Viv got back to the apartment, she found Justin and me in a...compromising position. That's it. That's the story. The dirty truth. Viv took one look at us and went straight to the closet to pack her things. That was the end of her relationship with Justin, and with me."

I couldn't breathe. Sweet, generous Bubbles had cheated with my father! Mom didn't cause the BFF breakup, after all. They hadn't talked in sixteen-plus years because *Bubbles* screwed up. No wonder Bubbles consented when Mom called last week. No wonder Bubbles was being so nice to me. She felt guilty!

"Oh, Lord," she moaned. "Please say something."

"Which one of you made the first move?"

"Who knows? No, that's not true. It was me. We'd had this incredible day together—talking, drinking wine at lunch, laughing. He held my arm when we jaywalked. I lost myself. He was getting me a glass of water in their tiny kitchen, and when he turned around, I kissed him. We were still kissing when Viv walked in. Oh Lord, couldn't you just murder me? You and Viv and Justin might be together right now if I hadn't…"

My stomach started to churn. She was right. If Bubbles hadn't double-crossed Mom, I might have had two parents and a shot at a normal life, instead of the constant moving and scrounging and changing schools. If Bubbles hadn't ruined Mom's life, Mom might have had the strength to follow her dreams in a constructive way. I might have known the man who was my father. I might even have liked him.

"You have every right to be furious with me," Bubbles said.

She was right about that too, and I *was* furious. Too furious to speak.

"I'm a monster, and I know it." She clasped her hands to her face.

What did she want me to say? *No, you're no monster, Bubbles. You're a good person. You were just in a tempting situation. It's not your fault that you wrecked my life and my mother's. No problem at all. Let's just forget it ever happened.*

"You know," she said, "I didn't even know Viv had a child—had *you*—until that phone call last week. We hadn't talked in all those years. I wrote letters and left messages, but she never got back to me. I nearly died when I found out, all these years later, that she'd been pregnant when Justin and I had our...thing. I nearly fell apart and died."

It made sense now, what George said about Bubbles going nutty when she got Mom's call. It wasn't just *Hi Bubbles, can you do me a favor?* It was *Hey, did you know I was carrying Justin's baby when you seduced him? No? Well, why don't you spend a couple of weeks with the proof?*

I was pretty sure that if I opened my mouth, it would be to attack Bubbles with every four-letter word I knew, so I kept my mouth shut. Bubbles apparently saw this as a good sign. She downed the last of her drink and said in a lighter voice, "I'm so glad Viv has found someone new. She deserves it. So don't be too upset with her now that she's finally fallen in love again. Won't you try to forgive her?"

I could not forgive my mother for towing me to Idaho any sooner than I could forgive Bubbles for splitting up my parents. "Look, Bubbles," I said, standing up, "it was kind of you to take me in this week, especially with it being the holidays and all. So thank you. I have to go now." I walked out of the room without a hug or even a goodbye.

I needed some air.

After throwing on my jacket (and noticing that George had made my bed before leaving the room), I ran downstairs and out onto the front porch, cursing myself in the bitter blackness for forgetting my mittens. No matter, really. I was broiling—with rage. Rage against Bubbles for betraying Mom, rage against Mom for ruining my life, rage against Starla for messing with Blue, and maybe even a little bit of rage at Blue for deserting me.

I pulled my hood up over my head and walked to the railing. The moonlit snow twinkled and rippled below me like a silver ocean. God, it was cold out, and so quiet I could almost hear the moon nudging across the sky. After soaking up the silence for a minute, I scooped some snow off the railing and made a ball in my bare hands. I threw it as hard as I could and listened to it thud, not so far away, on the ice. As it crackled and rolled into oblivion, I had a thought that so surprised me, I had to say it out loud: "My poor mother." Then with numb hands and tingling toes, I went back inside to pack and say good night to George.

I sat with George in the study for a while, then headed upstairs, but I didn't go straight to my room. Instead, I stopped at the Tiger Lily door and knocked lightly. "Starla, are you there?" No answer. "Good news, Starla—I'm leaving. Tomorrow. And I'm moving all the way to Idaho. Just thought you'd like to know."

I looked over to the Foxglove Room, Blue's room. I took a step in that direction, and another. Then I turned and went to my own room. Starla would tell him the good news soon enough. I was beat.

Hey, you've got to hide your love away.
—*The Beatles*

It was two in the morning, and I might still have been asleep if my belly weren't growling so loudly. But I hadn't eaten since Christmas breakfast, and my body was making demands, so I decided to make a quick kitchen raid. Just something easy from the fridge, I told myself, some cheese and bread or fruit and crackers. If I'd been less ravenous, less weary, or less scattered, I might not have dared to leave my room in the middle of the night. But I was famished, worn out, and pretty much topsy-turvy, so I forgot to be afraid. I simply got up and headed downstairs.

In the parlor, the only lights still on were the ones strung around the Christmas tree. I stepped over to the tree, where a dusting of pine needles covered the floor as if to signal that the holiday was officially over. And what a holiday it had been. The awful news from Mom. The luminous afternoon with George. Bubbles' toxic disclosure. There was no doubt about it—I needed chocolate.

As soon as I turned toward the kitchen hallway, something went careening across the parlor floor. I jumped back. Looked in all directions. Whispered Starla's name. I couldn't see or hear anything. Then, squinting at the floor, I found a tree ornament, a round one with tiny bells inside. It must have fallen earlier, and I must have kicked it accidentally. *That's all, just a decoration. Get a grip*. I picked up the ornament and headed toward the hallway.

"What?" came a crackly voice maybe twenty feet in front of me.

I froze, staring into the black hallway, my temples pounding, not knowing whether to run or confront. Then the hall light went on, and I saw Vincent standing there. He was—I couldn't believe it—he was in a bathrobe, barefoot, skinny-legged, closing Rita's bedroom door behind him. He was leaving Rita's bedroom! I dropped the ornament, which jangled to the floor.

"Shhh!" he whispered, fiercely flailing his hands. "She'd curl up and die if she knew you knew."

"I'm sorry—I was just hungry."

"Well, come on then. We might as well go to the kitchen. I suppose I have some explaining to do."

"You don't have to explain a thing," I whispered, but he was already holding the kitchen door open for me.

"I know," he said, following me in, "but I'm going to tell you anyway. It's better than having you guess." He took a stool and crossed his exposed legs self-consciously. "Go ahead, grab whatever you want."

"Are you sure, Vincent? Because I could just take a handful of crackers and disappear upstairs."

"If there's any of that tiramisu left, give me a helping too."

I found the tiramisu in the fridge, took a couple of forks, and decided not to bother with plates. Setting the dessert between us, I sat down and waited for him to take the first bite, which he did with gusto.

"Did I mess up your world?" I asked, poking my fork into the cream topping.

"You didn't even mess up my night. As long as we can keep this a secret."

"Don't worry about that—I'm out of here tomorrow. That's what my mother was calling about this morning. I'll be out of your hair, out of everyone's hair, in a few hours."

He put down his fork. "I thought you were planning to be here for a while yet."

"Plans change when they depend on my mother."

"Damn shame. You're good for this place. Good for Rita." He pushed the dish toward me. "Here, eat."

I took another forkful.

"All right," he said, tightening his bathrobe belt, "let me tell you what you've already figured out. Rita and I are…"

"An item?"

"Well, yes. But it's much more than that."

"So you're in love?"

"Very much so. For a long time now."

"How long?"

"Since about Rita's second week here."

"Wait, it's been that long and it's still a secret? Even from Bubbles?"

"Bubbles is usually too—how shall I say—distracted to pick up on such subtleties."

"You mean drunk?"

Instead of answering, he got up to rinse the dish off in the sink. "Just as well she's oblivious," he said. "She might not approve." He turned off the faucet and reached for the dishtowel.

"So what?" I asked, joining him at the sink. "So what if Bubbles disapproves? It's not like you're kids and she's your mother."

"No, but she's our boss, and we're living under her roof, and we need to keep in good standing. Rita says Bubbles would watch us like a hawk if she even suspected."

"She's right about that," I said, remembering how Bubbles acted when she saw me in George's bedroom.

Vincent finished drying the dish and set it in the drying rack. "Listen, Penny, I'm afraid I'm leaving at the crack of dawn to take Bubbles to an appointment on the mainland."

"Oh, right, I'm keeping you up. Sorry."

"What I mean is, this is probably goodbye."

There it was. *Goodbye*, that lousy word I was going to be saying a lot soon.

"So anyway…," he went on.

"Can I ask you one question first?" I said.

"Shoot."

"Did you once make Rita a casserole out of tuna fish and potato chips?"

"Rita told you about that?"

"Sort of. No details. She didn't mention your name or anything. Not that I didn't try to force it out of her."

"She was recovering from the flu one winter," he said. "Finally got her appetite back, and that's about the only thing I know how to make. That and fried eggs, but she doesn't like eggs."

"Well, she loved the casserole."

He smiled broadly. "Truly?"

"Truly."

We hugged then, but he didn't say that rotten terrible word, and either did I.

By the time I got back to my room, something got me

thinking about Bubbles in a different light. Maybe it was the talk with Vincent, maybe it was the fuller belly, maybe it was resignation. Whatever the reason, I started feeling the beginnings of forgiveness. I mean, sure, she did a bad thing to Mom. But did she really deserve full blame for what happened with my father? It takes two to tango. If The Donor was so easily seduced, he must have been prone to roaming. Maybe he'd cheated on Mom before. Maybe he'd have kept on doing it. How happy would Mom or I be living with that?

Realizing that I had to do something to fix things with Bubbles, I dug my pen and notebook out of my duffle bag, flipped past "The Purple Agony" pages, ripped out a sheet, and started writing.

Dear Bubbles,

I just want to say that, regardless of what happened in Chicago sixteen years ago, I am grateful to know you and to call you my friend. I think my mother feels the same way.

Thank you so much for taking me into your home this Christmas. I hope I wasn't too much trouble (although I'm pretty sure I was).

With love,

Penny

There. After folding the letter in half, I left it on my nightstand so I'd remember to slide it under Bubbles' bedroom door tomorrow. I fell asleep for a while after that. It was daylight when I woke up, time to break my news to Rita.

Chapter 12

I've turned my life around.
I used to be depressed and miserable.
Now I'm miserable and depressed.
—David Frost

"Just drink it," Rita said.

"But it smells awful," I complained. I was lying on the bed in her sparse, monkish room, and she was standing over me with a steaming cup. That's what I got for looking "like an unripe banana" when I stumbled into the kitchen for my morning coffee. I'd spewed the news of my exile to Idaho, and when I got on a coughing jag, Rita had me flat on my back with a pillow under my feet before I knew what hit me.

"It is just tea," she insisted, her voice so warm, so open, I wanted to tell her everything else—about the ghosts, about the murder attempts, about not being able to find Blue, not even this morning, even though he must have heard the news from Starla by now.

But I couldn't tell her any of those things, so instead I said, "It smells like medicine. Or cabbage."

"I put a few special herbs in it, that is all. Drink. It will help you."

I did need help, no doubt about that, plus I was too

exhausted to protest any longer, so I lifted my head and let her pour a little into my mouth. It was strong but not unpleasant. I took another sip. It actually tasted good—sweet and pungent—sort of like *pain d'amandes*, or Belgian hot chocolate, or was it praline fondue? Definitely nothing like the way it smelled. I wondered for a moment if Rita had ever nursed Vincent in this way, in this room, on this bed. Yes, I could picture them like that, being a couple together, being intimate. But of course I'd never let on that I knew.

"Good?" she asked.

"Good," I said, dropping my head back onto the bed.

She sat on the side of the bed and held the teacup on her lap. "Now tell me," she said, "what is really so bad? Okay, so you are leaving earlier than you planned. That is only a problem because you had a much better time than you bargained for, no? And you will come back this summer. What is so bad?"

"I don't know. For starters, how am I ever going to deal with Idaho and a new instant family?"

"You did pretty well with your new instant family here. You can do it there too."

"Rita, you might as well give up," I said, turning on my side to face her. "If you think I'm going to go skipping and singing to Idaho, you're wrong."

"You do not have to dance and celebrate, but you do not have to be sick over it either. You, who are so used to moving around. Now drink," she said, and I did. It went down hot and slightly thick. I felt a little better.

"Look, I'm sorry for being whiny," I said. "It's just, I don't know. The time I've spent with you, it's felt more like home than at home. And even home isn't going to be my home for long. God, Idaho!"

Rita got up and walked to the other side of the bed. "You know, I think this place has felt more like home to everyone since you have been here." She pulled out her nightstand drawer, took a small red box from it, and came back to her place next to me. "I want you to have this."

"Not another gift."

"Just a small memento, that is all."

I sat up, and she set the box on my lap. Inside, I found five picture postcards that showed off different Islemorow attractions: the beach in summer, a cliff overlooking the sea, fishing boats, a bike path through the woods, and of course the Black Butterfly.

"I started putting this together a few days ago. Of course, I thought I had more time, but anyway, these pictures will help you remember the island. And the flip sides will help you remember me."

I turned the postcards over. Each one had a recipe handwritten on it—brandied mango chutney, *pain d'amandes*, tiramisu eggnog trifle, artichoke hearts with risotto, and Rita's coffee. It was like a diary of our time together. Brandied mango chutney—that was from my first meal here, just before I met her in the study. The *pain d'amandes* was our first project together in the kitchen, followed soon after by the hunt for the artichoke hearts. Rita was making the trifle—and I was eating her chocolate—the day after my second dream journey. And of course Rita's special coffee was my hopeless new addiction—who ever would have figured she put aniseed and cardamom in with the coffee beans?

"I hope you will add your own special recipes to the box," Rita said. "That is what this is for, for your own special recipes and the memories that go with them."

"Thank you, Rita, so much," I choked. I placed the postcards back in the box and wiped my eyes. Just then I became aware that George was calling my name out in the hall.

"She is with me," Rita called back.

"Sorry to interrupt, but we've got to head out of here pretty soon."

"George?" I said weakly. I wasn't ready. I needed to say more to Rita. I needed to find Blue. I needed more time.

He said, "We've got to allow time for the ferry and the car ride to Machias, plus parking and security."

"Go," Rita said. "Go be with George. Go see your mother. Maybe you will write to me." She stood up, and so did I. We hugged tightly.

"Thank you for everything. And for the tea. I think it helped." I wanted to tell her I loved her, but I was crying too hard.

❦

Another turning point, a fork stuck in the road...
—Green Day

George was waiting for me in the parlor, the Christmas tree lights twinkling behind him. "Ready?" he asked.

"No."

"I have the van warming up. It's bitter today."

"Bitter is right."

We walked through the parlor and on into the lobby, where George held the front door open for me. "Go ahead," he said, and it was only then that I realized I'd stopped in the threshold. I felt like I was about to jump out of a spaceship with no spacesuit or tether cord. Who in their right mind would take that plunge without a push?

When I finally took the last step out of the inn, the arctic air grabbed me by the throat. My impulse was to run straight back to Rita's snug room, but George was holding my arm, and the humming van was just a few feet away. We hurried down the steps and jumped in.

While George rummaged through his pockets for his ferry pass, I turned to look at the Black Butterfly one more time—the gunmetal garrets, the charcoal gables, the pale icicle lights. The first time I saw that façade, barely a week ago, I was a different person. Back then I thought the world was black and white, not silvery grey. I thought people were either all good or all bad, wholly alive or completely dead and gone. I didn't believe ghosts existed. My most frightening experiences had been vicarious, in the stories I read. I'd never been in love. Never been torn. Never had a true friend. I'd been sleepwalking.

I had to look away.

When I turned back around, Blue was standing outside my window, just inches away. God, I wanted to talk to him! I wanted to leap out of the car and tell him how happy I was to see him. I wanted to ask him his plans. Thank him. Tell him why I was leaving. I reached for the door handle, but Blue shook his head. He placed his hand on my window and nodded. I knew what he wanted me to do.

I pressed my hand to the window, directly against his. It was the closest we'd ever get to touching. I closed my eyes and tried to feel him, to feel heat or pressure or any sensation at all. I couldn't feel a thing.

But I did hear something. Drum beats. Softly at first, barely perceptible above the sound of George's hunting around for the ferry pass. Then louder, more insistent, until the beats were a desperate plea inside my head. I felt shaky and somehow blurred. I think I tried to call George's name, but nothing came out. And then I was gone. *We* were gone—Blue and me.

We were standing outside on a summer evening, the sky deepening into bold purples and greens. In front of us hung a thick haze, or was it a curtain? Whatever it was, it made it impossible to tell where we'd landed, or when. Blue shut his eyes, and I followed suit, although it made me feel unnervingly wobbly. "Hold steady," Blue said—or maybe it was the drumbeats talking—so I planted my feet and waited for whatever came next.

I didn't have to wait long. A hot wind picked up from nowhere, spinning around us and howling so loud it drowned out the drumbeats. I couldn't have kept my eyes open if I'd wanted to, the gales were so powerful, so hot, so oppressively hot. Then, just when I thought I'd melt, the furnace blasts abruptly stopped.

"Oh," I heard Blue say.

I opened my eyes. The mist was dissolving, and we began to see what was in front of us. We were standing on a lush lawn ornamented with topiaries and flower-lined walkways. A croquet game was set up near a fountain. Adirondack chairs dotted the grounds. It was quiet, peaceful, and I dared believe this dream journey had taken us to a magnificent garden for our goodbye. Everything was so lovely, so serene—that is, until the last curtain of mist lifted, and a mansion came into view. It was on fire.

This place, these grounds, this mansion, suddenly felt familiar. With the drums beating faintly in my head again, I knew where I was. The Legacy Resort. The place where Blue had met his death, his imprisonment, his impossible task.

On the outside, the mansion still looked intact, but on the inside, I knew it was collapsing. Velvet wallpaper and brocade curtains were blazing. Crystal chandeliers and diamond-paned windows were shattering. People were choking on smoke, panicking, scrambling for their children. And all I could do was look on.

An instant later, throngs of people started spilling onto the lawn. Most of them were streaming out the front doors, but a few were climbing out of the windows. Everyone was wild-eyed and shrill. The smaller children seemed to think this was exciting, and they started to dance and do cartwheels in their nightshirts until their mothers pulled them away. It could have been a night circus if it weren't so deadly. Then I saw him. His caramel skin and his jet hair. He was on a crowded second-floor balcony, dropping terrified children down to a group of men who caught them in an outstretched blanket. He was alive, not ghostly. He was a real 21-year-old man, not a century-old specter of one. He was my Blue.

The drumbeats quickened, and the flames climbed. On the lawn, families clambered to find each other, babies cried, men futilely aimed garden hoses at the burning mansion. Despite the chaos, everyone looked angelic in the surreal light of the inferno, their faces glowing with the relief of escape, of taking that first gulp of the cool night air. Blue wasn't among them though. Of course he wasn't. He wasn't going to make it out.

We watched the windows burst, the roof crash, the smoke swallow the treetops. I wanted to reverse time. I wanted the smoke to fall off the branches, the roof to rise, the jigsaw pieces of glass to reassemble themselves into windows, the flames to squeeze back into that one cigarette in the dining room. I wanted it to revert to the way it should have been. But that was impossible. This had all already happened. There were no do-overs.

Suddenly a shout on the lawn rose above the uproar. Someone was calling, "Is everyone out? Is everyone all right?" I squinted into the crowd until his image emerged. It was Blue! Glassy eyes, wild hair, his body swaying. He kept walking up to the other men and asking if they had anyone left inside, but they wouldn't listen, and with each snub his voice grew more frantic.

The next voice we heard was a woman's scream. "Noooooo!" she wailed. "No, no!" She was running toward a man hunched over a blanketed bundle, sobbing. Everyone cleared a path for her.

"My baby!" the woman bellowed, grabbing the bundle from the grieving man. "My boy!" She lifted a corner of the blanket and went white, collapsing to her knees and pressing the bundle to her face. A limp arm fell out of the blanket as she shuddered.

Blue raced to the woman. He knelt beside her and bowed his head. "I'm so very sorry," he whispered. "So very sorry." But she didn't hear him. He tried to hold the baby's hand, but he couldn't do it. He stood up and talked to the father for a long time, but the man was oblivious. Finally, defeated and despairing, Blue simply staggered away, beyond the crowd and into the woods bordering the lawn.

Instinct told me to follow him, but somehow I was rooted in place, as if an invisible hand was forcing my attention on the newly childless couple. I hated being tied to puppet strings, and I struggled against the unseen chains, first with small tugs of my head, then with desperate jerks of my arms and legs. It was no use. I was stuck, and I was going to miss whatever was happening to Blue in the woods.

But here's what I didn't miss. Here's the thing that was going to be much more crucial: the stocky maid who plunked herself down on the grass next to the crying mother. Of course, I didn't know then that she was going to make everything change. I thought she was just the sideshow, the anti-climax, so at first I paid her only partial, grudging attention.

"Now darling," the maid said with a brogue, "what's the trouble here?"

The mother only cried harder.

"Come, let me see now," the maid persisted, reaching for the bundle, which the woman refused to relinquish. "Now look here, mum, I've had seven babes of me own and raised half me nieces and nephews. If you've a peck of sense in you, you'll let me examine this child." She said it with such force, such assurance, the woman relented.

The maid uncovered the baby boy's fair face. Harumphed. Put her ear to his face. Swung him over her shoulder and rubbed his back. Laid him on her lap and lifted his chubby little legs. Lightly rubbed the side of his neck. The baby's head fell to the side and his lips parted, a thin stream of blood trickling out of his mouth. Then he coughed.

He was alive!

The mother froze. She seemed frightened, as if she were looking at the ghost of her dead baby, as if she'd already shrouded and buried the child only to have him show up at her doorstep. She didn't know what to do, how to react.

The maid, however, was unfazed. "There you go, darling," she said, handing the boy back and standing up. "He just got a little too much smoke, is all. Made his breathing shallow, put him to sleep. Might've bumped his jaw, as well, but don't you worry. You've got yourself a strapping one there."

The baby gazed starry-eyed at his mother. Then he took a deep lungful of air and belted out the sweetest, loudest cry his parents had ever heard.

Only, Blue hadn't been there to witness it.

I had to tell him. I had to find him in those woods and let him know the baby hadn't died in the fire. The baby was safe and sound with his parents. Everything was all right. Blue didn't have to save someone's life because he hadn't caused anyone's death. He was a free man. I couldn't wait to share the news.

Except that suddenly I was back in the van, my hand pressed to the window. Blue was still standing outside, and from his expression, so full of wonder, I knew he'd seen everything I had. He'd heard that baby boy pierce the air with his cry. He knew he was free.

"Bingo!" George said.

"Hmm, what? You found the ferry pass?" I asked, turning to him.

"Yeah, it slipped into the lining of my parka. All set now."
He put the van into drive.

When I turned back, Blue was gone. Really gone—I could
sense it. And I think I was glad.

The trouble is, if you don't risk anything, you risk even more.
—Erica Jong

We drove silently for a while, past naked trees and heaped
snow. The drifts on the road rippled with the wind, making it
feel like we were traveling on a milky river. I saw a boy on ice
skates shoveling snow off a frozen pond, while another, smaller
boy stood on the edge swinging a hockey stick. All of it, all the
colorless bare sameness of it all, reminded me of goodbyes. I
sank into my seat and ached.

Then George said, "You have to cover your eyes now."

"What, why?"

"Because it's a surprise."

I folded my arms. I wasn't in the mood.

"Oh come on," he said, dodging a fallen branch in the road.
"Humor me."

"Fine," I sighed and closed my eyes.

"Are you peeking?"

"Nope."

"Good. It won't be long."

It felt long though. I felt every bump in the road, every tap
on the brakes. "How much farther?"

"We'll be there in a few seconds." The van slowed, turned
to the left, edged forward and stopped.

"Can I look now?"

"Not yet." His door opened and shut, and then he was opening mine. "Okay, you can get out now, but keep your eyes closed."

"You're going to make me walk blind?"

"Don't worry so much. It's hardly any distance at all, and I've got you." He took my free hand and helped me out of the van. We must have been in an open space, because the wind was so fierce, I thought my face might shatter.

"I'm not going to last long out here."

He led me slowly forward. "Yeah, I'd have held off for a milder day if I could, but…"

"Don't remind me. Are we in the road? This feels like pavement."

"No, not the road. Keep going. Almost there." We went on for what felt like ten yards or so, then he stopped. "Okay, you can open."

I lowered my hand and blinked a few times. At first, I had no idea where we were. Then I saw George's old school off to one side. We were standing on a footbridge over a frozen stream. The kissing bridge! And it was just the two of us. Just me and George, his blue-green eyes flashing, his cherry cheeks dimpling, his breath making cotton ball clouds around his face. "I've been thinking about this all week," he said.

God, he was enticing, but I decided to play a little coy. "You never answered my question, you know," I said.

"What question?"

"The one about whether you've ever crossed paths with a girl here when no one else was around…and kissed her."

"I'm a footbridge virgin." Abruptly, he pulled me to

him and kissed me so tenderly and strong, my heart melted straight into my toes. A car drove by, but that didn't stop us. We stood there kissing in the cold bright air of the footbridge until he finally tore his lips away and whispered, "I'm going to miss you."

"Me too." With my head on his shoulder and our arms around each other, my mind was whirring. "I still don't know how I'm ever going to survive what's ahead of me."

"Maybe you'll surprise yourself. Eleanor Roosevelt said a woman is like a tea bag—you never know how strong she is until she gets in hot water."

"How did you know that?" I asked in amazement.

"It was printed on my tea bag that day we ate at the Grindle Point," he said, and we both laughed.

Maybe Eleanor Roosevelt was right. Maybe I could turn the impending upheaval into a point of strength—into a bargaining chip with Mom. I wouldn't grouse about the move or Rex or that boarding school *if* Mom would green-light the Islemorow summer. I could fake the compliant daughter routine if it got me out of the family road trip and into the Black Butterfly with George. I could put up with anything for that.

And then all at once it hit me—the understanding of what I needed to do, right now, right here. The knowledge that I couldn't wait forever—or even until the summer—to do it. The dread at the very thought of it. Suddenly my whole weight was leaning against George.

"Penny, are you okay? Let's get you in out of the cold."

"I'm fine. I just realized something. Something I have to say."

"Okay, but let's do it in the car. Your lips are blue."

"Good idea." I was going to need to sit down for this one, and so was he.

We went back to the van, and George turned on the engine for some heat. I absentmindedly flipped on the radio, then shut it off.

"George," I said, but nothing more came out.

"Do you want me not to look?"

"What?"

"I thought it might be easier for you to talk if I weren't looking."

"Nothing is going to make this easier."

He reached across the cup holder and put his hand on my knee. I cleared my throat.

"George, I—what I mean is…" It was so hard to string words into sentences.

"I'm listening." He was holding my hand now.

I allowed myself a long moment to soak up the irresistible allure of his eyes. How I loved the way he studied me! How I feared the possibility—no, the probability—that I might never see that look on him again, not after what I was about to tell him. Then I just said it. "George, there are ghosts at the inn. There really are."

His hand went limp in mine.

"It's not what you think—or thought. Mom didn't send me here to prowl around. And I wouldn't have done it even if she'd asked. I don't—didn't—believe in ghosts."

George was a study in perfect stillness. I waited for him to exhale or cough or lick his lips, but he didn't. He didn't do anything.

"But then I met them, two of them. Two ghosts. Down to one now."

He let out a long breath, as if he were trying to blow my words away. His eyes were different now. Sharper. Darker. Colder.

"It's true. I saw them. Talked to them. I don't know why I can see and hear them and you can't. Mom can't either, by the way. Just me."

He looked down at our twined fingers. Squeezed them.

"I'm sorry, George. I know I'm rattling your cage here, but it's true, it really is. Do you believe me?"

Silence. Then, "No. I don't know. No." His face was all pain.

"Oh." I started to take my hand away, but he wouldn't let go.

"Penny, no. Look, I don't know what you think you saw. All I know is, I almost lost you once already when you fell off the pier. I'm not going to lose you a second time, not if I can help it, not just because you believe in…Jesus, Penny, it sounds so crazy. If I could just see one of them, you know? Just one glimpse. One solid shred of evidence."

"Carl Sagan said the absence of evidence is not evidence of absence."

"Carl who?"

"Sagan. He was an astronomer."

"Oh." He traced the outline of my hand with a slow, attentive finger, as if he were searching for a Braille message on my skin. "Look, I can't promise I'll ever believe in ghosts. But I believe in you. Can that be enough for now?"

"More than enough. For now."

I kissed him then—his lips, his temples, the little scar

on his eyebrow, the corner of his eye—not caring that I didn't know what lay in wait for me tomorrow or next week or this summer. In this moment, I was with George. I'd lobbed the first bomb, and he still wanted to be with me.

Snow started falling, melting at first on the warm windshield, then dusting it white. We kissed until there was half an inch of snow on the windows, and then we kept on kissing. It was probably nearly time to get going to the ferry, the place we first met, but neither of us said anything. Not yet.

I could have stayed here just like this until June.

Chapter 13

Here's to words that tell the truth
When it's easier to lie.
Here's to staring into the sun
When you should close your eyes.
—"Untangle Me" by The Maine

We pulled into the small parking area by the wharf, and,
just like on the night I arrived here, ours was the only car
there. We could see the ferry chugging its way toward shore,
spitting smoke and chopping the water. "Looks like we've got
a couple minutes," George said, turning off the ignition and
unbuckling. He took my hand and leaned toward me—I think
we were going to pick up where we'd left off—when suddenly a
man was standing right outside of George's window. I gasped
and grabbed George's hand tighter.

George turned to see what I was looking at. "Hey, it's
Buddy," he said.

"Buddy?" I asked.

"From the Grindle Point Shop, remember?" George said,
winding down his window and letting the polar air inside.

I guess I didn't recognize Buddy out of context. Plus, he
wasn't smiling and animated and rattling on about baseball, the
way he was that day at the shop. In fact, he looked downright
solemn, and by the looks of the flimsy windbreaker he was
wearing, he was probably going numb.

"Hey, Buddy," George said, waving to him with the hand that held mine.

"Hey," he said glumly.

"Fancy meeting you here," George offered. "Where's your truck?"

The question seemed to puzzle Buddy. He scratched his cap and looked around the parking lot. He opened his mouth as if to say something but only shrugged. George glanced at me with a raised eyebrow.

"It's cold out there," I said through George's open window. "Why don't you come in and warm up?"

Buddy looked at me hard, as if trying to grasp the meaning of my words but not quite getting it. "I...I..." Now he was staring off in the direction of the ferry.

"Are you all right, man?" George asked. "Here, let me help you in." He let go of my hand and was about to open his door when he stiffened, letting out a kind of cough-gulp before going silent.

"George, what's the matter?" I asked.

When George turned to me, his face had lost its rosiness. "Where did he go?" he asked.

I looked up at Buddy, who was shaking his head. "Who?" I asked.

"Buddy," George said with an agitation I hadn't heard from him before.

"He's right there," I said. I took George's hand again and pointed out his window. "See, right there."

"Uh...oh," George said. "I, I don't know what happened there. Buddy, did you...?"

Buddy blinked back at him, and the two of them just stared each other down while the van turned into the Arctic Circle.

"Okay," I said, "I don't know what's going on with either one of you, except that you're both probably hypothermic. Buddy, you stay there, and I'll help you into the car." I kissed George's hand lightly before opening my door.

"Jesus!" George shouted as I stepped out of the van. "What the hell is going on?"

Now I was the one getting agitated. "What?"

"He's gone again," George said. "Look. He's just…gone."

Buddy leaned against George's door and stuck his head inside. "I feel the same way you do, pal," he said softly.

A feeling of dread and astonishment jumped on my chest. Buddy had something wrong with him, and I knew what it was. George had something wrong with him too, or maybe something right—though I could scarcely believe it—something bad and good at the same time.

"What's going on?" George repeated, more quietly this time, like a mantra, not like a real question.

"George," I started, my eyes still on Buddy. "George, this is incredible but…" Wait, no. I had to be completely certain first. I'd already freaked George out enough for one day. I didn't want to add to the mayhem unless I was absolutely sure.

I walked around the front of the van to where Buddy stood. He pulled his head out of the window and blinked at me blankly. "It's okay," I told him, and then tried to rest my hand on his shoulder. My hand fell right through him. This wasn't Buddy. This was Buddy's ghost.

"What are you doing?" George asked me.

Good question—what *was* I doing? I didn't want to put George through this, and yet it might be the only way to get him to accept the truth. Then again, did he really need to confront reality now, in December, a full six months before I'd be back to stoke Starla's vengeance? Still, if I didn't do this, George would have to learn about Buddy's death through the grapevine, and then he'd put two and two together and figure out that we saw Buddy *after* he died. I didn't want George to be alone when he found out how the universe really works.

I sucked in some of the icy air. "Take my hand, George," I said, reaching my hand through the open window. As soon as we made physical contact, he jumped, his eyes darting from Buddy to me. Now there was no doubt: George could see Buddy's ghost *as long as he was touching me*.

"What happened to you, Buddy?" I asked.

Buddy stood up a little straighter. "So you can see me, hear me? No one on the ferry could."

I glanced at the ferry, which by this time was only a hundred yards or so from the dock. "What happened out there?"

"I don't exactly know," he said. "I was coming back from my sister's on the mainland, just sitting in my pickup, fiddling with the radio, and, I don't know, my head started pounding like hell all of a sudden, like sheer hell, and I got woozy, and, and...I don't know. All at once nothing hurt anymore. I felt okay, so I got out of the truck to say hello to Thaddeus and Cliff, and they just ignored me. Only, I don't think they were ignoring me. I think they really didn't know I was there. And then, I don't know, here I am with you."

"My God," George breathed.

Buddy shifted. "Am I...dead?"

I didn't answer, and neither did George, but we didn't need to. Buddy knew the answer to his own question.

"What do I do now?" he asked, lost.

"I think," I said, "I think you go back to your body. You go back to it, and then you'll be able to cross over."

"Cross over," he said, his eyes brightening a little. "Cross over, yes, that's what I need to do. But how...?"

"No idea," I confessed. "But I'm pretty sure you'll know. When you're there with your body, you'll know."

The ferry, carrying five or six cars and trucks, bumped against the dock with a thud. "I hope you're right," he sighed, then smiled dimly. "Well anyway, there's not much to lose at this point, is there? So long, Penny. So long, George."

George couldn't speak, so I said goodbye for both of us. "I'm sorry," I said as he turned to go.

"Me too, sort of." Then he was gone.

Oh, what a tangled web we weave when first we practice to believe.
—Laurence Peter, misquoting Sir Walter Scott

If words existed that could comfort George, I'd have used them, but there weren't any. All I could do was climb back into the van and sit with him while he struggled to take everything in. Ghosts are real. He can see them when he's touching me. Buddy is dead. There was so much for him to absorb, so many assumptions to discard, so few notions left to hold onto, and no words to do the revelation justice. Absolutely none.

I sank into myself. Part of me was terrified that George

would resent me for forcing his eyes open, but another part of me felt relief not to be alone with this otherworldly world. I wondered if it only worked with George, or if anyone I touched could see a spirit. Wait—yesterday when we were exchanging gifts, didn't Bubbles put her arm around me when Starla came downstairs? Yes, and she asked me if I was feeling faint. Rita came over and put her arm around me too. Neither of them had a clue that I was gawking at the ghost of George's birth mother. So it didn't work with just anyone. For whatever reason, it only worked with George. We were entangled.

The blast of horns on the ferry jolted George and me from our separate trances—not the ferry's own horns but the horns of the cars on board, all honking.

"I think," George said, squinting at the ferry. "Yeah, the first truck in line is Buddy's. No one else can get off because he's blocking the way. They don't know he's…"

I could see Buddy again, standing next to his pickup, looking inside, probably looking at his slumped body. A man with a beard came out of the pilothouse and rapped on Buddy's window, probably telling him to wake up and head out. Finally the man opened Buddy's door and leaned in. A moment later, he was pulling out his cell phone and shouting for the other passengers to help. Buddy looked on as a handful of men lay his body on the deck.

They were probably going to try CPR while they waited for an ambulance. Hold on, did the island even have an ambulance? I didn't know. All I knew was that any efforts would be futile. Buddy was already dead.

"That ferry is going nowhere," George said. "Those are

Buddy's good friends on board. They're going to stay, and it could be hours before a medic can get here. We might as well go back home, try again tomorrow."

Not exactly the way I wanted to finagle some extra time. I sighed and let my head fall onto the seatback.

"Besides," George added, starting the ignition, "I need to meet this ghost you say is hanging at the inn."

The dead can be more alive for us, more powerful,
more scary, than the living.
—Jacques Derrida

Oh no, oh no, oh no. That's all I could think on the ride back to the inn. I wasn't ready for this, not yet. The idea of introducing George to his own mother—to the girl who wanted me dead— was more than I could handle. But there was no way out. I couldn't deny George access to his birth mom any sooner than I could make him un-know about ghosts. This was the moment of truth.

We parked in the driveway, but neither of us made a move to get out.

"Is there anything I should know first?" he asked.

His question was so loaded it almost made me laugh. There was so much he should know, but it didn't feel like my place to tell him. What if Starla didn't want George to know she was his mother? Should I even care what she wanted? My only concern was for George…but I didn't know if he'd be better or worse off if he knew the full story in all its pain and misery.

"Penny?" he said.

"We might not even be able to find her," I said. "She can hide. She can go places."

"Okay, so it's a female," he said. "That's one thing. What else?"

"She's young. I mean, she was young."

He nodded.

"She hates me."

"Why?"

I shrugged. "Because I can see her."

"So she'll hate me too?"

"No."

"Why not?"

"I-I just don't think she will. No one could hate you."

"Well, there's only one way to find out. Let's do this thing."

"Okay," I said, "but can I use your cell first to text my mom? I don't feel like talking to her right now."

"Sure." He pulled his phone out and showed me what to do.

"Ferry not running," I typed aloud. "Will try 2morrow. Will let u know." I pressed Send. "There," I said, handing back his phone. "She can't argue with the ferry, can she?"

"You ready then?"

Hardly, but I got out of the van anyway. George came around and took my hand.

We stepped into the lobby, which felt strangely quiet without anyone puttering around. Bubbles and Vincent were stuck on the mainland, and Rita must have been back in the kitchen or her room. "Follow me," I whispered. "No talking." I had the feeling Starla would take cover if she knew I was around.

Hand in hand, I led George upstairs to the Foxglove Room

and motioned for him to open the door. The room was empty. We tried the Tiger Lily Room next, but that was vacant too. I had to wonder if she was even in the house.

"Should we try the other rooms?" George mouthed.

"Are any of them unlocked?" I asked.

"Not since last summer," he said. "Except for yours."

"Let's try downstairs," I said.

No ghosts in the parlor. Same for the dining room, the study and the kitchen, including the crawlspace. Rita's room was locked. Maybe Starla had hitched a ride with Bubbles and Vincent this morning. Maybe she wanted a change of scenery, or maybe she wanted to hide out on the ferry so she could get me there. Maybe the universe was telling us this wasn't the time for a mother and child reunion.

"Attic?" George asked.

That was a possibility, I supposed, although it was the only floor where I hadn't encountered Starla before. "Okay, yeah," I said, and back we went, through the parlor, up the winding staircase, down the hall, up the second, narrower staircase, onto the third floor.

Bubbles's room was empty. Empty and pristine—her bed was made with military precision—although I couldn't help noticing a lipstick-stained wine glass on her night stand. None of my business really.

"Maybe we should try the cellar," George said, running his hand over Bubbles' dressing table.

"What about your room?"

"It's locked."

"Why?"

"Habit, I guess."

"Since when?" I asked.

"Since I've lived in a dorm."

"No," I said. "I mean, how long has your door been closed and locked?"

"Since I left it this morning. Why, you think she went in there last night? To watch me sleep?"

I shrugged. He shuddered. We left Bubbles's room and crossed the hallway to George's door. He had to let go of me for a moment while he jiggled the key with one hand and turned the knob with the other. He gave the door a quick, hard push and stepped inside.

She was there. Standing in front of his open closet, reading the story it told. She lit up when she saw George, but when I followed him in a second later, her smile crumbled. Then George found my hand, and when he clapped eyes on her, I felt his legs buckle. She was staggered too. She knew he could see her. She could see it in his stare, his shock. Her mouth fell open, and she looked to me. No one spoke.

George was the first to break the silence. One word. One simple, stunning word. He said, "Starla."

He said her name!

"Wait, you know who she is?" I said when I recovered enough to speak. How could that be? I thought the adoption was closed. There was supposed to be no way for him to know.

Starla looked astonished, thrilled. Of course she did. Her son was looking straight at her for the first time ever, and he even knew her name.

"Yeah," he said, riveted to Starla. "You look just like your picture."

Picture? What picture? How did he get hold of a picture? I absently put my hands to my face. George quickly took my hand back.

"So," he said, gazing at Starla. "It's really you." He took a step closer, with me in tow, and then another. He reached his free hand toward her, then stopped.

Starla moved her hand to his. They couldn't touch, but they tried. Their fingers slipped through each other's, then hovered nearby.

They put their hands down. "I can't believe this is happening," she effused. "I can't believe you can see me, talk to me." She glanced at me, and for a flash of a second, I thought she was going to thank me for bringing her together with her son. What was I thinking?

"You look so young," George said.

"Sixteen," Starla said. "That's how old I was when I...you know."

"How?" he asked. "How did it happen? No one told me anything. Was it because of me—because of the pregnancy?"

"Of course not," she said. "I think someone drugged my soda at a party, and I must've had a reaction. I'd've died whether or not you were on board."

"Jesus," George murmured.

"Yeah," she said.

"I have a thousand questions," he said. "I...is it okay if we sit?" She nodded, and he walked us to the bed, where he perched on the edge. I had no choice but to sit down too.

Following his cue, Starla sat cross-legged on the desktop. "Okay, fire away," she said, "but first answer one question for me. How did you know my name and my face? That woman didn't tell you anything about me."

"That woman?" he asked.

"Bubbles. Ma. Whatever you call her."

"Oh," he said, shaking his head. "No. Oh—she did give me this though." He pulled the crescent moon pendant out from under his shirt. "Your parents wanted me to have it, I guess."

Starla nodded. "I wore that every day."

"I still do. Anyway, your parents wanted me to have something else too. They put together a box of stuff, your stuff, for me to have. Only…"

"Only what?"

"My mother never gave it to me. Don't know why."

Starla crossed her arms. "I do."

"Yeah, well, I found the box one day when I was snooping around her room to see what she got me for Christmas. I must've been around ten or eleven." He looked at me here and added, "We used to do the regular kind of Christmas presents back then, the kind where you go to a store and buy stuff."

I nodded and put my other hand around his arm.

"I found a couple of video games, an iPod, and then this white box under her sofa. I thought it was another gift, so I opened it up. On top was a note from your mom—I guess that's my grandmother. It said…I don't know, how grateful she was that I was getting a proper home, and that even though this was a closed adoption, she wanted me to have something of my birth mom to hold onto, stuff like that."

"Really?" Starla looked surprised. "My mother never got

flowery like that when I was alive. I guess death changes people. What else did she say?"

"Nothing I can remember. She just signed her name with big curlicue letters. Audrey."

This made Starla laugh and clap her hands. "Now it all makes sense. Audrey isn't my mother. She's my sister. We were close. So what was in the box?"

"Let's see. A Beatles CD, a fancy barrette, a couple of friendship bracelets. But the most important things were the photos. A photo of you as a baby and a photo of you just the way you are now," he said. "I used to lock myself in that room and stare at those pictures for ages. Especially the one of the older you. You're wearing a University of Maine sweatshirt and holding a lit sparkler."

"I remember that picture. It was the Fourth of July—summer was always my favorite." She sighed. "Audrey did a pretty good job with the Starla-in-a-box project. Okay, your turn."

George repositioned himself on the bed. I could feel his muscles unwinding just a bit. "First of all, who's my father?"

"I was afraid you were going to ask that," she said. "You aren't supposed to know, you know. It's not like you could go knocking on his door saying you figured it out."

"I know, but I just need to know, for myself, to put an end to all the wondering."

She uncrossed her legs and let them dangle over the side of the desk. "Okay, all right, his name was Bryan, and he was my chemistry teacher."

"Teacher?" George asked. "Was it...did he...did he...?"

"What, force me? No. He was gorgeous and brilliant, and

I'd had a thing for him since biology class. He's who you got those beautiful eyes from, from a thirty-year-old man who would have lost his job if anyone found out, and since I loved him, I never told anyone."

"Wait," I broke in. "Didn't your parents demand to know?"

"Yup." Starla didn't break her gaze with George, and she directed her answer to him. "I promised to fess up as soon as the baby arrived. I had no intentions of making good, of course, but I figured I'd cross that bridge when the time came. Which it never did."

George didn't care about Starla's parents though. He cared about his father. "So, about Bryan. Did he step up? Did he at least stay with you?"

Starla turned toward the window.

George's face withered. "Oh. I...sorry."

"It's fine, really. It didn't change anything in the end."

George let out a shallow breath. "Maybe and maybe not," he countered. "Maybe if he'd been there for you, you wouldn't have ended up at the kind of party where jerks drop dope in your drinks."

"Or maybe he'd have talked me into getting an abortion."

I tightened my hold on George's arm. His muscles were knotted again.

No one spoke for a while. Starla stared out the window, and so did George. Finally George said, almost to himself, "I just can't believe it. I mean, I always thought..." His eyes moved to Starla. "So you, like, followed me here?"

"I wanted to spend some time with you," she nodded. "I wanted to see you grow up."

I felt a slight shudder pulse through George. "Okay," he said, "so…what exactly have you been doing all these years? I mean, have you been…?"

Good. Here was the creeped-out tone that Starla's stalking warranted. George had to be wondering if he'd ever been alone in his life, ever had one truly solitary moment. Or was he always watched, like a prisoner under continuous surveillance? He had to suspect it now, that whenever he thought there was just one person in the room, there were two, and when he thought there were two, it was a threesome.

Starla didn't comprehend the extent of her trespass, or else she was hiding it. In any case, a smirk of amusement tiptoed onto her face. "I didn't follow you into the bathroom, if that's what you mean," she said. "I just hung out in the kitchen while Rita taught you to cook. Watched you learn how to ride a bike and drive a car. Listened to your bedtime stories."

"All day long?" he asked, working my hand so hard it hurt.

"Not exactly," she said, sliding from the desk to the chair. "I did meet someone here. Someone special. I spent time with him too."

"Right, Penny told me there was another ghost. Where is he now?"

Starla's smirk evaporated. "I don't know. I haven't seen him lately. He may have left. For good." She shot me a glare.

George looked to me and back to Starla, probably trying to decipher the mutual daggers. "What is it with you two? Penny thinks you hate her."

Starla didn't respond.

"Well, do you?" he said.

"I'm not her biggest fan."

"Why?"

"Yes, why?" I dared her. It was all I could do not to blurt out the real story, the hateful, murderous, true story. But she was George's mother, and maybe he was still trying to find a way to accept her, so I didn't say a word.

Starla drew her knees up to her chest. "It's complicated, George."

"Is it because she lets me see you?"

"No—"

"Maybe you don't like that I can tell when you're around now." He said it without a hint of emotion, a perfect poker face.

"You're wrong," she said.

"Then set me straight." But was he challenging her or trying to help her out?

When she didn't answer, he said, "Did you do anything? To Penny?" She still said nothing, so he turned to me and asked, "Did she do...anything?"

Starla stood up. "George—"

"She tried to kill me," I said, and the kid gloves were off.

His face blanched. I could almost see the wheels turning as he ran the week's events through the lens of this news. "When you almost drowned," he said, scarcely audible. "That's when."

"And again when I was out with Vincent, when you were getting your haircut."

"It wasn't like that, George," Starla pleaded. "It's not like that."

George lowered his head for a long moment. When he raised it again, the color was back in his cheeks, and they were burning. "God, Starla, what did you do, push her off the dock?"

I answered for her. "No, she can't push people. She rigged the dock. It was all premeditated."

The flame moved from George's cheeks to his temples. "And the van?"

"Stowed away in the trunk and took over the wheel," I said. "Tried to steer us off the road into a ravine." My heart did the cucaracha in my chest as I remembered my near-annihilation and how Starla had laughed in delight at it.

George looked at me with glistening eyes. "And you couldn't tell me because you knew I wouldn't believe you."

That was true, but I didn't want to acknowledge it. This was painful enough without laying a guilt trip on him.

"George, please," Starla begged. "You've got to understand."

"I do," he said. "I do understand."

But what did he think he understood? George stood up, pulling gently on my hand. Together, we walked across the room, stopping within a pace of Starla, and he said to me, "There's something I have to say." I blinked. He turned back to Starla and said, "There's something I have to say."

She looked up, hopeful.

He inched closer to her and said, "Leave."

With that one beautiful word, the roof came off and the sun poured in.

Starla fell back against the desk. "No, George, please! I love you. You're my son, my everything. I'm your mother."

"I already have a mother," he said matter of factly. "Look, I'm sorry you died the way you did, but after what you've done to Penny, you are nothing to me. I don't want you around. Go cross over like you're supposed to."

"But I can't!" she moaned. "Penny, tell him I can't. I know Blue explained it to you."

Damn! She was going to make me back up her defense.

"Tell him," she implored.

I rubbed my chin.

"Tell him!"

"All right, all right," I consented. "She's telling the truth. She needs to be near her remains to cross over, and she doesn't know where they are."

"Okay, fine, don't cross over," he told her. "But don't stay here. I don't want you anywhere near me or Penny. Not ever… what do you mean, remains?"

Starla started sobbing, so I explained, "It's your corpse. Or your skeleton or ashes. Just some part of you."

"My parents had me cremated," Starla managed, "and they kept me on the mantel. I used to visit the box of ashes sometimes. But one day the box wasn't there. I tore the house apart and no box. It was gone."

George narrowed his eyes. "Gone, just like that?"

"Then I remembered," she went on. "Audrey once told me—this was back in, like, middle school—she wanted to be buried in a flower garden. I told her I wanted to be scattered over the Atlantic." Her voice trailed off. "It's a big ocean."

George seemed to be thinking deeply about this. "So that's why you sent Buddy back to his truck," he finally said to me.

I opened my mouth to speak, but Starla wasn't going to let the conversation veer away from her. "George, don't shut me out," she choked. "I can't cross over. I won't have eternity with you. This is my only time." The way she said it, even I felt a twinge of pity for her.

"No," George said.

"I'm begging you!"

"No, I mean, you *can* cross," he said. "That baby photo of you. On the flip side there's a lock of your hair. That's part of your body, so that'll work, right?"

Starla stared dumbfounded at George. "My hair? This whole time?" She forced a smile and a sigh that was supposed to suggest relief, but I knew better. I knew she was even more wretched than I'd given her credit for.

"You!" I growled.

"Did you hear that, Penny?" she said in a fake sweet tone. "George knows where a lock of my hair is."

"And so do you," I said. "Blue told me how it works, how you can feel it if any of your remains are nearby. You lied to Blue about it so he'd feel sorry for you. And now you're lying to George for the same reason. You are so messed up."

Starla shrank back. "But I...I..."

"No, no more excuses," George said. "You are going to either cross over or find another house to haunt—you choose— but either way, I'm going to watch you leave."

She stood up. Pushed the chair under the desk. Fanned her teary eyes. "And if I choose not to do either of those things?"

George didn't bat an eye. "In that case, I'll destroy the lock of hair, and then you really never will cross over. Not even when I'm dead and gone from here."

She gave a nervous laugh. "Well, when you put it that way. You win then. Penny wins too. Congratulations to both of you."

"Stop it," George said. "Just follow us."

I was afraid she was going to run away, but she didn't, which I guess made sense. After all, her one and only chance to cross over was in Bubbles's room. Her sole hope of seeing George or Blue again was in that room. She had no choice but to tag obediently along with us.

"I've never been in here," she said when we got to Bubbles's bedroom. "I never had much interest in that woman."

"That woman is my mother," George pointed out. He let go of my hand while he retrieved the memory box from its hiding place under the pink sofa, the same sofa where Bubbles told me the truth about her and Mom. Then he sat on the bed and lifted the lid.

Starla, her eyes fixed to the box, stepped toward George. Maybe she just wanted to take a peek at her memorabilia, but maybe she had a scheme. I wasn't going to take any chances, so I ran over to George and looped my arm through his so he could see her. Two sets of eyes were better than one.

George pulled out the photo from its plastic sleeve. She was a cute toddler, I'll give her that, all yellow curls and oversized eyes. There was no guile, no attitude, no hint of the ghost she would become. Just a happy little kid.

Starla inched closer, and as she did, George instinctively tightened his grip on the picture. "Hold on," he said.

"Sorry, I was just wondering," she said, "wondering if I could see the barrette you mentioned."

George frowned.

"I know which one Audrey would've put in there," she said. "I got it for my first semiformal. I used to love that thing, that's all."

He looked at me for advice, but I didn't have any. He sighed and dug out the barrette, which was shaped like a butterfly and studded with black rhinestones. A black butterfly. After turning it over between his fingers for a minute, he tossed it to her. "You can keep it," he said.

Starla caught the barrette and immediately put it in her hair. When she did, something melted away from her, and I could almost see the excited girl who was getting ready for her first dressup dance.

"This sure brings back memories," she said dreamily, her eyes half-closed. "My dress was black silk, backless, and I had butterfly earrings too. They played 'What a Night' and 'Forever Young' and they turned off the lights for 'Dance with Me.' My feet were killing me in those four-inch heels, but I didn't care. It was wonderful." When she opened her eyes, they were misty.

For some reason, I reached over and touched the lock of hair taped to the backside of Starla's photo. It belonged to a girl who'd once had a real life and real princess dreams. A girl who was denied that life and those dreams through no fault of her own. A girl who was long dead, but whose hair still felt fresh and supple. I pulled my finger away. George detached the lock.

"Here," he said to Starla. She walked over to accept it, but George took it back. "Hold on, just a second," he said, dividing the lock in two. "Okay, here you go. Just, you know, in case."

She took the half-lock in her cupped hands. For a long time, she simply peered at the yellow strands, mesmerized. Maybe she was trying to remember what it felt like to have a living body. Maybe she was trying to recall what it was like to be a two-year-old. Or maybe she was just stalling.

Finally George said, "Do you...know what to do from here?"

She looked up at her son. Nodded slightly. Tried unsuccessfully to form a convincing smile. Blinked. "I wish you a long life, George. Long enough to give you time to forgive me."

"Goodbye, Starla," he said, a little bit compassion, a little bit command.

"Goodbye." She held the lock tightly in one hand and smoothed her hair with the other. The black butterfly barrette fell to the floor with a light ping. And she was gone.

🦋

First things first, but not necessarily in that order.
—Doctor Who

George eventually picked up the butterfly barrette, which looked small and childlike in his hands. He ran his fingers over the black rhinestones. It was still real, still solid, not vapor like its owner.

"So," I asked, "do you think you'll ever forgive her?"

"I don't know," he said, his eyes trained on the hair piece. "I don't know if I should."

"You should."

He looked up. "Why?"

"Because. Because she can't hurt us anymore. And she's your mother. And besides, they say forgiveness is the best revenge."

"I'm gonna need some time on that one." He sat beside me on the bed again and picked up the white box. "Funny how Ma never showed me this."

"Yeah."

"I wonder what Starla was thinking. She was so sure she knew Ma's reason."

I looked in at the memorabilia. "She probably figured your mother was jealous."

"Of a dead girl?"

"Of a girl who shared your blood."

He shook his head. "I don't think that's it. Why would Ma have given me the moon necklace then? I think she was trying to protect me from finding out how young Starla was. Like it would be harder knowing I was the result of some backseat high school fling than a respectable mistake between adults. The necklace, it's real jewelry, it could've belonged to anyone, but this, this is all kid stuff."

I put my hand on his thigh. It felt good to touch him just to touch him, not to make him see a spirit. "I hadn't thought of that," I said. "I'm guessing Starla didn't either."

"Probably not." He put the barrette in the box and closed the lid, then got up and deposited it unceremoniously under the pink sofa. "There," he said. "All done."

"*All* done, really?"

"For now. Come on, let's go downstairs. I need to get out of here."

That was the best idea I'd heard in a while. We closed Bubbles's door behind us, took the narrow steps to the second floor, and headed down the hall to the winding staircase. As we passed the Lilac Room, George said, "I can tell you one thing. I don't care if I ever see another ghost again."

"That might not be possible if you're with me, you know."

He stopped. "Are there any other ghosts I should know about?"

"Not that I'm aware of. But you never know."

"Well," he said slowly, "I'd say we're a pretty good team if we need to be. I'm not worried." He kissed me lightly, then tilted his head toward the Lilac door. "It's still yours for a night," he said. "Do you want to…?"

Of *course* I wanted to. But all at once, the irresistible aromas of Rita's magic glided in. I took a deep breath, and I could smell it all—everything sweet and savory, rich and airy, potent and mild, exotic and familiar. The bouquet was spellbinding, like a command that somehow feels like your own idea.

"Hey," I said, "How about first we…"

"Excellent idea," he agreed.

We kissed one more time and headed straight to the kitchen.

About the Author

SHIRLEY REVA VERNICK'S interviews and feature articles have appeared in *Cosmopolitan*, *Salon*, *Good Housekeeping*, *Ladies' Home Journal*, national newspapers and the publications of Harvard, Johns Hopkins and Boston Universities. She also runs a popular storytelling website, storybee.org, which is used in schools, libraries, hospitals and homes all over the world. She lives in Amherst, Massachusetts.

In 2012, her debut novel, *The Blood Lie*, was named to the American Library Association's list of Best Fiction for Young Adults. It received the Simon Wiesenthal Once Upon a World Children's Book Award and was an Honor Book for both the Sydney Taylor Book Award and the Skipping Stones Award.

Other Books by Shirley Reva Vernick

REMEMBER DIPPY

"An enjoyable and provocative exploration of the clash between 'normal' and 'different' and how similar the two really are."
—*Kirkus Reviews*

THE BLOOD LIE

"A powerful—and poignant—reminder that no person can live freely until all people can live freely."
—Lauren Myracle, author of *Shine*